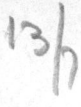

A WALK IN THE SUN

Tall, mean Tobius Harris, gunfighter and bounty hunter, had a code—be prudent, but don't back off from man or beast. A loner riding the no-name trails, his name sent a shiver down the spine of many a murdering renegade. On his way back from fighting Redskins at the foot of the Rockies he crossed trails with Ringer and Bender, a pair of vicious outlaws who killed slow and hard. They left him for dead and stole his horse, leaving him to become prey for a crazy sect living deep in the Colorado mountains. Only by using his strength and ingenuity could he escape and ride a bloody trail to wreak his vengeance.

A WALK IN THE SUN

E. Manklow

Lansdown

CHIVERS·PRESS·BATH

First published in Great Britain 1987
by
Robert Hale Limited
This Large Print edition published by
Chivers Press
by arrangement with
Robert Hale Limited
1992

ISBN 0 7451 5570 7

British Library Cataloguing in Publication Data available

A WALK IN THE SUN

CHAPTER ONE

Tobius Harris, bounty hunter, one-time Pinkerton's Agent, Indian scout for the army, sure is a good mixture. Been wintering in Fort Belver, having given some time to Colonel Ronald Ashley, on account he'd had more trouble than he could rightly handle, keeping the Comanche Run open, so-called by settlers, freighters, prospectors, making for the mining camps, fledgling towns, the Oregon Trail and ranchers, pushing their great herds along the vast plains to Dodge, Wichita, Ellsworth, Abilene and other boom towns.

Yep, was rough for 'em all, even a web of forts huddled along the belly of Texas to the Brazos River wasn't no match for Chief Quanah's warriors.

The staked plains of west Texas being no more'n a Devil's playground, on account them red devils played Hell's hide-and-seek with the hated white eyes and some of Colonel Ashley's half-tried troopers wasn't no match for 'em, burning, pillaging, massacre'ng, all over, if I hadn't been sniffing along for a coupla no good renegades, on account a thousand dollars reward, alive or dead, preferably dead. Butch Osman and Sam Bready, trading whisky and guns to the Comanche for stolen cattle and horses. I wouldn't have been in this 'ere territory, was four of 'em, but a drunken shoot-out way back in Shutters Creek, a fleapit of a place some fifty miles south had left these two laughing, only there wasn't much to laugh about when I cornered 'em, just mighty surprised at meeting their Maker with their boots on. Busy branding cattle when I caught up with 'em, about ten miles from the North Fork of the Red River. Nice and cosy in a neat hollow, just pale fingers of smoke curling upwards, told me this near empty territory was being peopled by two-legged critters. Had spied pony droppings, unshod imprints and deeper prints of shod horses, telling its tale of Comanche and whites, movin' a week back along the South Canadian River, a hopeful sign on account there hadn't been any rain to wash 'em away, all telling its own tale of serious business between 'em.

I reckon them renegades' noses and ears was so full of the stink of sizzling hides and bawling cattle and their brains working overtime at the notion of them wads of dollars nesting in their pockets, had made them a mite careless, having no look-out, they had to be quick and be gone.

Thickset, beefy, bull necked, their wide backs bending over the kicking cattle, cursing the bawling bolt eyed beasts, the heat, the flies, their strong hands holding the red hot brandin' irons. They sure hadn't got any spares to reach for their hardware.

I didn't wait to call 'em out, just shot 'em like rabid dogs, having in front of my mind the mutilated bodies of screamin' whites, scalped heads of young troopers and wagon trains of terrified eager eyed folk snaking along for a new life in a new world.

I'd just laid their corpses over their mounts set on making for the nearest fort, when I met up with Ashley's patrol.

They came riding down that steep grade, their horses foaming, legs splayed out, trying to get a footing on the loose noisy shale.

I reckoned they was a bunch of scavengers, on account their ragged dusty sweaty uniforms, stubbly faces hidden under low-brimmed hats, made a solitary critter reach for his gun.

A closer look showed they was troopers, led by a youngish critter no more'n thirty years old.

They was bloodied and tired, their red rimmed eyes showing no interest in my corpses, drawing small clouds of flies over their raw fleshy holes, on account they had a coupl'a their own, the naked bloody scalped heads, thick with flies, bouncing against the horses' hides like red balls, wetting their dusty uniforms, trickling through their fingers.

The youngish critter opened up, licking dry blistered lips, squinting through dusty, caked eyelids.

'I'm Colonel Ronald Ashley,' he gave me, his

sharp eyes no less knowing, on account of the dust in 'em, 'been two weeks hounding the Comanche and Arapaho, you got a coupla whites?'

'Yep,' I said, 'coupl'a no-good bastards, Butch Osman, Sam Bready, gun-running with them red bastards you been skirmishing with.'

He gave a tired smile. 'Makes sense,' he said, 'needn't bring 'em in, top them into the scrub, I'll sign the note. You got a name, or perhaps you prefer me not to know, bounty man?'

I bristled a mite, sayin' 'Yep, got a name, Tobius Harris, Tobe, been Indian scout and Pinkerton's Agent.' I was for going on explaining my virtues when he showed more interest.

'Have heard. Seems you, Scout Abel, a Dog-face halfbreed, helped the army put the fear of the Devil into the rampaging Sioux way back in the Black Hills. Pleased to make your acquaintance.'

I took an instant liking to him, as we stood under the blazing sun, smelling each other's stink. He went on, 'We got a war going on with the whites too. Caught the Comanches busy with them three days out. Them white bastards had a wagon load of guns and whisky, we didn't get a peep at them, they had a look-out perched up in the rocks.' He gave a rueful grin, addin' 'All we got was the wagon and a few dead redskins; sometimes you win, more times you

4

lose. I guess my men are real tired out. You're welcome to come to the fort, be glad of some of your knowhow.'

And that's how it was, sure feel right proud at having met up with him, yep, right proud.

Got a few critters like him to line up with. My pards, Will, Joshua, Old Sod, Abel, Dog-face, reckon I learnt a lot from 'em all, one way and another.

Josh, I can't just go all the way with, on account he believes in the Lord, which I can't quite cotton on to, him being born into slavery, damn near whipped to death, taken from his own folks and having to keep alive in a white man's world of hatred, cruelty and such.

Me, I ain't never had no truck with the Lord, on account I've been in partnership with the Devil long as I can recall.

I can see Ashley now, straightening up in the saddle as we neared the fort. A fine looking critter, strong jawed, steady eyed, no nonsense, dark curly hair straying out from under his hat, his tired half-smile showing strong even white teeth and a boiling hatred of the redskins, burning out of his dark eyes. The sorta critter a man would think twice about making an enemy of; a tough ruthless fighting man, young enough to see sense and getting enough wisdom to use it in this land of lust, lawlessness and violence, growing as fast as the grass, trees, forests and raw fledgling towns springing up all over. Yep,

5

quite a man, no quarter given, none asked, never expecting more of his men than he could do himself. Didn't ask 'em to be dust-free, with shiny buttons glinting on their uniforms. Their unkempt straggly hair, tattered duds, hanging off their bodies sure blended in with this harsh, cruel, unrelenting territory, like a critter has to take up the challenge of it.

The sudden flash storms, blistering heat, flies, freezing winters and the everlasting threat of the redskins.

I'd been with him since last August, scouting along the staked plains, the Red River, keeping 'em on the move, giving 'em no time to sit and take comfort that their murdering pillaging days were near over, on account the first fall of snow had showed.

I'd left the fort and been on their tail, following their sign for a coupla days and sighted 'em about five miles from Death's Head Canyon, so called because any critter peering down into its evil depths would be like looking at dozens of black eyeholes and yawning mouths slashed up the sides. Jagged knife-edged rocks waited down below, holding bones of four-legged animals and two-legged whites baking in the sun. I sure struck lucky, 'cause I spied a second camp holding spare horses which told me they was still raiding. The rocky area of empty stream beds wiped out their tracks and I figured they was all a hundred

6

miles from their villages which didn't worry 'em none on account they could do that distance almost without food and water, just getting a lick here and there.

The October sky had showed more'n a promise of snow, and let a few flakes down as a kinda warning. A thick blanket would fall almost overnight and them murdering bastards would need them spare horses.

Ashley's patrol was over a day's ride away and I was hard put to reason it out, them bastards could be gone time I brought the troopers here.

I stayed high up between the pines, oaks and cedars watching 'em fingering the piles of white folks' clothes, coloured dresses, hats, shoes, pots and pans, shovels and whisky.

Then I reckon the Devil done me a right good turn, 'cause them red devils got drunk, dancing and yelling round their fires. Come dawn they lay like dead meat; the fires smouldered to grey ash, nothing moved. I counted four of 'em and was all for sneaking down and slitting their throats when a tight bunch of 'em rode out of the close brush and started the fires going again. I allow there was now about sixty and best I could do was meet up with the patrol.

I hightailed it out, rode my roan hard, and next night I met Ashley. We talked as we rode, drank from our canteens, ate dried jerky, cursed the heat and flies. About a mile from the second camp we rode real careful, hugging all cover, not putting scary birds tangling up in the high blue sky. It was then we met up with another curious critter. He just stood there, like one of them buffalo shaggies, a .45 buffalo gun held right careful, his tall body half-hidden by thick broken rock. When he sort'a figured out who we were he came out.

A giant of a hombre, towering over me and I'm all of over six feet of bone and muscle, about two hundred and thirty pounds. Thick bearded, red haired, grey eyed, wide bodied, strong as an ox, he walked towards us, then I recognised him under them red whiskers—Nat Pearce, Indian Scout.

'Well I'll be doggone if it ain't old Tobe, you ornery son of a bitch, reckoned on you bein' dead, what the hell you be doin' in these 'ere parts?' he said, his mouth wide open in a huge grin.

'Might ask you the same,' I said and gave him a run down on what I was about with Colonel Ashley, he not at all surprised at coming across another scout, more right glad about it.

It seems Nat had been tailing them Comanches for over a hundred miles, really after sniffing out what their chief was up to, but the slippery bastard seemed to be everywhere at the same time.

'Reckon we'll clean that bunch out then,' he

settled for, ''cause they're still pourin' that rotgut down their throats and snow is beginnin' to show itself, they'll be hoofin' it back to their villages, settle down for the winter not venturing too far out.' He snorted, grinning at some secret thoughts, adding 'That's where the army comes in, ride in on a winter's night, slaughter the lot of 'em.' His gruff voice grew hard, his grim face set like stone and there was a whole lot of hate in his eyes. I had an understanding of him; his wife had been raped and murdered, his place burned out by raiding Comanches and a whisky-peddling white bastard, a black bearded critter, Rufus Larkin. Nat just went missing for a coupla weeks, then rode back into town with the bastard's head on a pole, stood outside the sheriff's office, kicked the door open, dragged the half-asleep lawman outside, dared him to take it down 'til it fell off of its own accord, then left the town.

Went Indian scouting, heard grizzly tales of his slaughtering, that he was still alive was a kinda miracle. Ashley's troopers shook their tired bones together as we spied the horses bunched up in a neat shady clearing. A small creek ran like a silver ribbon, feeding the coyote willows hugging the banks, their silvery leaves playing in the water. A few Comanches lounged about, a right pretty peaceful place, broken by the roar of a buffalo gun, spitting rifles and screaming horses. One by one, the ponies lay kicking in their death throes, a terrible sight. Nat and Ashley grinning at each other, as the bloody slaughter went on. In a few minutes the redskins and ponies lay in a welter of blood and clouds of flies homing in onto the warm flesh.

The same at the other camp, we just rode in like dusty yelling red eyed devils, pumping lead into the whisky sodden bodies.

Nat taking the lookouts all quiet, slitting their throats, then propping 'em up between the rocks, silently laughing at his bloody handiwork.

We hadn't lost a trooper, had given Quanah a kick up the ass, which he wouldn't be forgetting, 'cause he had plenty of spit left.

Nat stayed with Ashley. Two of a kind, needed for this lawless land.

I was glad for all white folks and last I saw Ashley a coupla weeks back, was him riding out with his men, now the ice had begun to melt, early spring breaking out all over, hell-bent on wiping out them redskins and Nat prowling like a demon God, going where no man wanted to be, like his life was one long vengeance trail, his sights set on Quanah.

Both of 'em smart enough to know that the red man has a built-in knowing and want for fighting, them being suckled on the harsh bitter milk of this vast untamed land.

CHAPTER TWO

I loped along, sniffing the odours of springtime, sweet smelling juicy grass, knowing the buds were popping open like cracked nuts.

All life was on the move, the great forests putting on their green, even small dried-out cactus and bunches of parched scrub would be showing something to tell a critter the long harsh winter was over. The frozen silence cascading into laughing silver, swirling water, filling up the empty river beds, gulches, wollows, making new streams, creeks.

The huge ocean of blue above, the sound of chattering birds, my roan's feet rattling on the rocky river bed. The warmth of the sun stoking up for the coming summer, putting its fingers down, sorta getting the feel of it, if you know what I mean, as I made for the other side, to make camp, brew coffee, made me a mite careless and when my horse blew softly and I felt his hide ripple under my ass I didn't have much time for what was coming.

Three Arapaho came hell for leather out from a clump of aspens, sitting on their wiry mustangs like they was growed on 'em, their legs gripping the foaming sides like another brown skin. I reckon I was right lucky, 'cause my roan's feet stood tight in the gravel whilst I put a shot between the first pony's eyes. It dropped like a sack of grain, its legs splaying out, its belly near bursting at the force of it, pinning the naked savage beneath it.

Wasn't no time for 'em to spread out, on account they'd ridden in bunched up close together, a way of riding they often did, reckoning on their yelling and hollering would put the frighteners on the white eyes. Me, being an old hand at their capers, wasn't in no way put out.

The bolt eyed beasts tangled together, screaming and bucking, shoving off the sweaty bodies. I aimed, taking their faces away, leaving only their black pebble eyes, grinning teeth and gushing blood soaking into the new green and a growing cloud of early spring flies, their eyes hardly open, homing-in on this unexpected feast. I moved right careful, hadn't reckoned on any of 'em raiding this far out so early, no doubt from a hunting party after fresh meat and had a notion of Colonel Ashley and Nat Pearce starting out on their endless war between the reds and the whites. Spied a jack rabbit, told my gnawing belly to quieten itself, crossed over the border into Colorado, rode for miles, seeing no sign of any human critters. Then smelt smoke, cooking meat and coffee and rode into a small arroyo, holding a long bearded prospector roasting a coupla jack rabbits.

He didn't show no surprise at a stranger

12

riding in, just grinned through his whiskers, his sharp blue eyes twinkling.

'You just came at the right time stranger, set to be done in the shake of a dog's tail.'

I must admit it was mighty fine meeting up with him after talking to my horse for so long and coming up against the redskins hadn't helped any, had only just got the hairs on my neck to settle down and my ears darn near stretched out of shape for listening. 'You been comin' far?' he asked, turning the brown greasy meat, making the drips send flames curling around it.

'Yep,' I answered, 'been scouting from Fort Belver, stayed over the winter, met up with some red bastards way back, young braves, not much reasoning in 'em, else they wouldn't be coyote meat now.'

He nodded. 'Them varmints pop up like gophers out of holes. Me and my pard Joe Wilks been prospectin' along Buffalo Pass, about forty mile from the South Canadian River, never found a trace of the stuff, he lost his hair before winter set in, reckon we got caught up with them buffalo hunters, thumbin' their noses at Chief Quanaha's Comanches and Arapahos, slaughterin' their buffalo by the thousands, laughin', like it was a game they was playin', to boast about it to them willin' whores in the saloons.'

He poked the meat and went on, 'Ain't

13

altogether blamin' them redskins, hell-bent on wipin' out them buffalo hunters, the greedy bastards had been killin' enough of them buffalo shaggies to keep all the skinners busy for months. Reckon over thirty thousand hides were shipped to Dallas, Kansas and other boom towns, in just a few weeks.' He nodded again. 'So the tribes got together, held a sundance around Elk Creek, along the Red River, prayin' to the Great Spirit for guidance, my pard got his hair lifted, a few skinners lost more'n their hair, poor bleedin' bastards. I was lucky, high-tailed it out of that territory, now I'm workin' on my own, ain't found any gold as yet,' he perked up a mite, 'still got all summer and them buffalo hunters will be at it again, same every year, ain't no stoppin' it, ain't that so stranger?'

I grinned, 'True, have heard Colorado is built on gold and silver, you make for Pikes Peak, Denver?' He nodded again, his eyes turning soft and dreamy, no doubt seeing them golden nuggets resting in his horny hands.

He rummaged around and came up with a bottle of rotgut, took a long swig, then another, belched and swallowed quick, so as not to lose it on account it floated on the meat and coffee we were busy putting down our throats.

I took a long gulp, snake poison at its gut rot worst, or best, depends on how you look at it. Sure had a startling kinda bite to it, felt like I'd lost my ass, didn't feel much of anything else, growing from my legs, my head kinda swelled into a jumping ball, blocking up my ears, then suddenly before I panicked, a lovely God-damn soft feeling crept through every part of my body, I felt light as them feathery clouds gathering above. I leaned back, letting myself get lost.

He laughed, showing a row of small sharp ratlike teeth, 'cause under his whiskers his face wasn't no bigger than an apple.

'Ain't it just somethin', my pard knew the makin' of it, God rest his soul; reckon he left me the best knowhow he had, always see him when I drinks it, natural I should. Ain't ever gonna forget him, poor bleedin' bastard.'

I nodded, still half-floating, saw his face bobbing about like there was several of 'em, so there we sat and was downright lucky no redskins were about, but he'd scouted out wide before making camp, having a knowin' of the land and the tricks it plays on a critter. That's why he'd survived so long, lean, leathery, tough as one of them buffalo shaggies' hides.

He sure was a living oracle of past happenings.

'Yep he'd met up and eaten with confederates on the rampage, since he hadn't got anything they wanted, he was left alone, yep they sure was a bunch of murderin' thievin' renegades. Got a likin' for their boozin' lawless ways, plenty of women, money, nothin' to anchor 'em down, yep he'd heard of Striker Reed's gang, real ripe they'd been, broken up now, Striker and his brother Cole, sorta just faded out, but a few of 'em no doubt ridin' in fresh territory.'

He leaned back against the burning rock, puffing out his stink, right overpowering on account I couldn't smell my own. 'Come mornin' I'm movin' on,' he said. 'I'm makin' for Denver.'

'Keep to the known trails, settlements and such,' I said. His sharp eyes raked over me.

'You ain't pannin' for gold, since you ain't got no corns on your hand, reckon you look mean enough to be a bounty man.' He shrugged. 'You got plenty of business goin', renegades, horse thieves, roamin' gangs, enough to keep you goin' till you're old as me if you live long enough. Last one I saw a year back had been dragged through scrub, cactus and such, just lay like raw meat off a hook in a butcher's shop, just his eyes had a knowin' in 'em, been left for buzzards and coyotes. I shot the poor bastard, only critter I ever shot.' He sniffed at the memory of it, adding, 'Course, I asked him first, reckon he was right grateful on account he hadn't got a bone in his body that wasn't broken, but it snaggles at me like a loose tooth, jumpin' now and then in my gums, then it comes right up in front of my mind.' His sorry hangdog face lit up again when I shoved over the rotgut. 'Right good this 'ere liquor,' he

16

wheezed as it dribbled through his whiskers.

I was real glad of his company, just us, the horses—no hate battling in our bodies, no vengeance to tear at us; been a long while since I'd been free of such thoughts.

When the night faded out and the grey of early dawn changed the colour of the territory and the rising sun pinked and blued the flanks of the distant thrusting mountains pushing up into the sky, we lit a fire, cooked beans, brewed coffee, rode a while, then parted.

I watched him vanish into the close green, heard his pots, pans and shovels rattling, then nothing. We'd met, passed the time of day, shared our victuals, yet we were nameless, just passing through critters who had no need of knowing or caring. It was the way of it.

Met up with buffalo skinners, strong, hard, seasoned critters, making for the South Canadian River, Texas Panhandle, the Red River.

Their wagons tight with .45 buffalo guns, ammunition and enough supplies for weeks. They wasn't gun-running, or whisky pedlars, just plain good natured skinners.

CHAPTER THREE

I kept moving right careful, no crushed grass or redskins' ponies' droppings showed.

Been all of a coupla years since I lost my wife Betsy, giving birth to our son Jamie.

The memory of it, like a raw living sore and it ain't going away, nor the sight of her pain-racked contorted body, waiting for old Doc Marsh, who couldn't make it after being taken by a murdering gang of Confederates from our little town Springville in Wyoming, they bent on losing themselves along the no-name trails, through the Black Hills where such critters slipped like evil ghosts—then left his gunshot corpse for coyote meat on account of a dead man wasn't going to put a posse on their tails.

I'd stood by her grave holding our boy, then closed the door on our four golden years we'd shared together, cleaned my hardware I'd stashed away with my hell-raising dubious ways; she having no knowing of it, never seemed the right time to tell her. Had settled down, like peaceable folks, getting hitched in that sweet-smelling new timbered church, feeling right good inside, best feeling I'd ever had. Reckoned it would last forever, but in a few terrifying hours it was snatched from me.

I got the dismals recalling it, smelling the land, wakened from its long winter's snoozing, alive, fresh and clean putting its best face on. I ain't got no illusions about its cruel harshness, just because it all looks kinda pretty, 'cause I know it's as grubby as yesterday's old newspaper. If there was such a God damn one in this 'ere territory.

Like I know the Devil is sitting on my tail again, same as always, gives me some ripe pickings then snatches 'em back again, letting me take a coupla steps forward, then finding myself taking four backwards, on account I've always had a kinda partnership with him. I shook myself, feeling the sweat trickle through my shirt, on account that blasted orb up there had fingered through it, gave a kinda hard grin.

The oldtimer's revelations had brought it all back—saw again that murdering bastard's face as I slowly tightened the narrow leather strip round his neck; seeing his face change colour, his eyes bursting, his tongue edging out like a pink animal escaping from a dark hole, and the memory crawling back into his dying eyes. Yep, I'd evened up for Betsy, Doc and myself.

I'd tracked 'em down after being caught up in the Black Hills fighting the raiding Sioux on account they got their tempers roused over the army building a fort in their sacred grounds.

We'd trounced 'em good and hard, ain't likely they're going to forget it, then I sniffed them renegade bastards out in their secret valley in the Wichita Mountains. Got myself accepted, rode with 'em, ate with 'em, slept with 'em and when time was right, choked the life out of the murdering bastard and high-tailed it out.

Still have a wondering about 'em all, 'cause they was all set for a bust up and now the oldster had let drop they'd broken up.

Yep, I'd carried a mighty lot of hellfire vengeance, boiling from my brains, to my ass, driving me through that long hot summer. Reckon my boy is growing some, got the makings of being a fine strapping lad. Turned my guts over when I last set eyes on him, laying in his cot. Saw Betsy looking at me, her eyes, mouth, hair and I'm going to tell him all about her, so he'll always have her in mind, 'cause I'm turned forty—won't always be around, but he's got a mighty fine family raising him like their own, my pard Will and Daisy.

Maybe I'll settle down again, being in the wood business with my other pard Joshua, getting it stacked high, filling them iron belly puffers tight with fat logs, gettin 'em roaring along them endless rail tracks, snaking across the land.

Reckon I got itchy feet, they just won't stay quiet, guess being a bounty man most years I can recall, cleaning up the foul miscreants, so folks can rest easy has kinda settled in my blood. Betsy sure anchored me down, now ain't got no reason for staying put and no matter how hard I arranged my future the Devil always turned it inside out, finding me more ways to use my time. Like now, walking in the sun, figuring on grabbing a fistful of 'wanteds' lining the timbers in sheriff's offices, 'cause all this territory's thick with murderers, renegades, horse thieves and such.

Don't need a circuit judge wasting his time when I'm around, lets him off for more upright, righteous activities. The sun was well up and roaring when I edged out from the empty flat waterbed of burning stones and sand, onto dry scrubland and kinda sparse for cover. Spied horse droppings, old and cracked, scuffed-up earth, all signs of wild horses passing through, and a waterhole not far off.

The wind had quickened, not just a whiff of hot air, bringing with it a trickling of sand from the blistering rocky terrain; felt it on my face, my eyes, nose holes. My roan blinked and fidgeted as if he knew he'd got to get a move on, find good cover and water, 'cause that wind sure had got a nasty bite to it. I searched for a hole or an empty mine, nothing showed.

Found some broken boughs, old split treetrunks, dragged 'em to a heap, the hot whiff became a whistling, howling demon, bringing clouds of sand with it; got my bedroll and, shouting all the profanity I knew, huddled in between the heap and waited for it to blow itself out.

It went as quick as it had come, leaving just a dirty yellowing sky, beginning to turn blue again.

My horse, being a kinda smart beast, had turned his ass to it and looked kinda sorrowful on account he had sand packed right up to his belly and the way he stretched his eyeballs at me showed he wasn't liking it no-how.

We got ourselves dusted off, wiping his eyes and mouth out before we moved on. He being smarter than most got them tired feet going and found the waterhole, sandy and brackish it might be, but sure a pleasant sight for sand-scratched eyes.

I threw off some of my duds and went in like I was in a bathhouse. He got in, head well down, reckoned he was laughing cause his tail was going like a piston in an engine.

I reckoned I was about forty miles from Buckshot, a fledgling town growing stronger on account of silver and gold strikes, like dozens more of 'em growing almost overnight, bringing hordes of homesteaders surging across the wide plains and Kansas prairies—opening up the vast empty land, filling it with the sound of rattling wheels, groaning oxen, profanity, picks and shovels, shouting at the iron hard ground as weary folk dug in, often using the flat sides of broken wagons to build a shack, call it home, then leave it to blow away in the wind, when

22

the railroads snaked away from the terminus in the Sam-Luis Valley; then opening up somewhere else, not even giving the place a name, just calling it 'somewhere else'.

Last time I'd been in Buckshot the whining winds coming off the ass of the Sierra Nevada had stripped it to near piles of timber and irate red-eyed folks, foraging for their possessions, were bunching up together hell-bent on putting it into shape again. Then the creek overflowed, damn near washing 'em out as a deluge of water from a spring and summer cloudburst sent it boiling through empty gulches, wollows, ending up in the main dirt street.

I reckon them redskins sure sniggered at the white eyes' stupidity settling down in such a place. They never got caught like that, being reared on the harsh brew the land dealt out to 'em.

I let my sweaty body sink back in the water, felt it creep up under my armpits, listened to the sound of insects, birds and my brain telling me what was in front. Buckshot, steamy coffee, chunks of red meat, rotgut, the bustle of leathery critters moving along the main street, horses pulling at their hitching posts, a barber getting my whiskers trimmed, a game of cards; the stink of it all, from pigs, rotting garbage to stale sweat—it sure was mighty appreciated, 'cause a lonely hombre needs to talk and listen.

I left the water to dry out on one of them

burning rocks; watched the mud settle, looked at my crooked feet that had been roasted by the Cheyenne years back when my pards Will and Joshua had snatched me from 'em, as we fought our way back from the Big Horn Mountains. They sure looked good, washed clean. Looked kinda odd, on account the sun never got at 'em . . . sure was a funny sight.

I shook the sand out of my duds, climbed into 'em, got a fire going. When my horse blew softly I cursed myself for not thinking straight, my belt and hardware between me and the waterhole. I made for 'em, feeling the rush of heat spread through my body that hadn't anything to do with that fireball up high.

'Won't make it,' grated a voice. I stiffened. I'd heard it before, back in that hidden Wichita Valley, Striker Reed's hideout. I turned, Ringer and Bender sat on their mounts, caked with sweat and sand, their guns lined up on my belly.

'Now ain't that just something, us meetin' up like this, figured you'd been caught in that gully when the mountain shoved off that load of rockfall and water and here you be, washed clean as a spring flower,' sneered Bender, adding, 'We found Buck, with his tongue hangin' out, his eyes boltin' out of his head. Face wasn't a good colour either, reckon he died real slow and hard and that ain't nice, sure ain't,' he spat. ''Course, we ain't a gang any

24

more. Striker and Cole broke us up, then just went after we had ourselves a shoot-up, Torn and Stu got killed. Seems the rot set in after you showed up and you was a ripe sharp sod, had all the answers, comin' from nowhere, goin' off into nowhere, like all the time you had a reason for comin', reckon you found him and killed him and now you ain't got your guns to take slithers of skin off a critter's toe, showin' us all how handy you was with 'em. Let's see how you shape up without 'em.'

My brain swivelled about in my head, my guts heaved, these ornery bastards roaming about, thieving and murdering, like ghosts from the past and Ringer hadn't forgotten as to how I'd drawn his blood, shooting round his big toe, telling him and the others how easy it was to being a dead man or a live one on account he kept his big mouth shut; reckon it will always gnaw at him like a hornet's bite.

They dismounted and came across, Bender's mean piggy eyes stared at me from a pock-marked brutish face, a wet fleshy mouth half-filled with black broken teeth stretched into an evil grin. Wide thighs strained out his pants like a second skin, his gunbelt near hidden under meaty folds of a barrel of a belly. Could still hear his boasting as to how he could snap a critter's neck with one hand like roping a steer and that he'd killed his first man at sixteen years old, just for the fun of it, in Austin

25

County, Texas.

Ringer, a vicious killer from Tennessee, a snakey grey eyed scraggy thinlipped sneering bastard, cold as a dead fish, his long front yellowing teeth—covered by slimy baccy juices and spittle—needed his long tongue for ever wiping 'em clean. He'd roamed and murdered along the Brazos River, the Pecos, Arkansas and New Mexico.

A close-mouthed sod, only after a bit of eager boasting he'd let out about raping little Mex gals in Mexico and other places. He glared at me, his small eyes wide in their sockets, his tongue lickin' and sucking at them teeth. I saw pleasure growing in his face, turning his eyes kinda glassy as a twitch moved the skin over his cheekbones. The pair of 'em hadn't changed; reckon they'd found a common link between 'em, wasn't on the cards they'd mellowed a mite.

Bender's great hands bent me backwards like I'd never had a backbone, a punch under my ribs laid me flat, heard the air puffing up out of my guts, saw the sky slipping about sideways, heard 'em chortling, my skin sorta crawled at the notion they'd dreamed up something special on account they hadn't killed me.

CHAPTER FOUR

The sky steadied itself, I smelt their stale sour sweaty bodies as they swirled my Colts, balanced my Winchester in their hands, looked my roan over, sniggering and spitting, shaking off some of the sand from their stubbly faces.

Bender reached for a broken thick bough, fingered through its gear and brought out a rusty nail.

'Always had a hankerin' to nail your hide to a fence,' he said and smashed his fist into my face.

Ringer straddled me like a bucking steer. I felt my sense begin to thin.

Bender spread my hand flat on the wood and with a hefty punch the nail went through.

The searing pain of it forced out a terrifying scream, I kicked and writhed, felt my mouth wide open, howling like a wolf, a beaten dog, wasn't no human sounds. The terrible splintering pain of it spread up my arm, through my body, yet my knowing never left me. I saw quite plainly their excited leering faces, the sweaty marks, beads of it dripping from their dust-caked flesh; their bright shiny eyeballs, long teeth, black broken ones, the deep pink holes of their throats. Their heads seemed to hover like on strings, bobbing this way and that.

'You look real fine Tobe,' sneered Ringer.

'You ain't goin' no place. Them buzzards and coyotes will be smellin' you out in less than a coupla days, we ain't hanging around to see the fun of it, but we'll be thinkin' of you, sure will, and seein' as how you won't be wantin' your fine horse, we'll just take him along, reckon he'll fetch a tidy handful of dollars.'

I felt and tasted a wet trickle of blood running from my mouth. I licked at it, found no loose teeth. The sky hung up there through a cloudy haze. Heard a grating sound coming up out of my guts, at the notion of them bastards riding off with my horse, my breathing quickened, felt a terrible fearsome panic reach into my brain. I tried to scream out, nothing came, only the same choking animal sounds being carried on the hot blistering air, then nothing.

The sun was paling when I came to, a wetness back of my head told me it had met with a hefty crack on the hard rock, and my shirt sticking to my back wasn't held there by all sweat, it was dripping blood. I looked at my hand, didn't look like a hand, more like a chunk of red bloody meat. It had swollen round the nail.

I tried to ease my body over, but the pull of it sent a spurt of blood washing through a thick barrier of flies and the searing pain of it reached all corners like my body was on fire.

My face, lips and eyelids had blistered under the sun's fierce heat, my eyeballs weren't focusing right.

Heard the hot breathing wind rustling through the trees, holding no moist air to cool my tortured flesh. I told myself the Devil sure had dreamed up another game to play and after another day, my hand a great mound of yellowing pus, I smelt the strong odour of coyotes as they edged round the waterhole, looking me over, heard the flapping wings of a buzzard, saw his great ugly curved beak, half-open, then yellow teeth, an underbelly brown and dirty, hooves planted near my head and it was the Devil. 'Kill me you devilish bastard, been on my tail long enough,' I croaked, felt my blistered lips tear as the skin broke, but he hadn't got that in mind. A trickle of water dripped over my face, my head, guttural voices and much movement, my body dragged into a shade, heard the coarse animal sounds welling out of my mouth as my hand pulled on the wood, more voices, I managed a squint, wasn't the Devil, a Sioux hunting party, led by an old grey-haired warrior.

My brain told me this was the end of it, they was for finishing me off, as one of 'em leaned over, an axe in his hand, to chop my face in half. I shuddered as it swept down, heard a sharp guttural voice, felt the metal thud on the wood, the jerk of it brought a howling scream, dying away to nothing, I floated in a sea of pain. The old Sioux leaned over, I smelt his rancid sour body, heard his voice from a great distance.

'White brother do this to white brother, white eyes sow evil seeds, not good either for red man. You will live and take revenge, you great warrior hold pain well, like red man ... me, Swift Foot, great warrior of many moons ago, have many battles, not kill weak white eyes, only strong ones.'

A mist came before my eyes as I saw their brown shapes ride off.

It was darkening when my senses came back. Shadows turned the close brush and stands of trees into mysterious shapes, even the boulders seemed to wobble and form into ugly faces, like I'd been pitched into another world of painful dreams and sweaty nightmares. I could only feel one side of my body, told myself I was dying, that it had all been a dream, my hand still nailed to the wood. I turned my head and looked. It was free, the nail like a small black baleful eye in a red bed of bloody flesh, my arm swelled up tight in its buckskin sleeve. I dragged myself to the water, deep rasping groans coming from me like a dying animal as my hand moved along beside me, a legless 'thing' that had latched itself onto me. I laid in the waterhole, the water creeping through my duds, washing out the stink from my body, the excrement from my flesh. Saw the 'thing' under the reddening water, still holding its unwinking piercing eye.

Must have lain for hours, the soothing feel of the water holding off some of the searing pain that racked my body; laid my head in the damp weedy edges, letting it flow under my chin. Saw the stars stacked up in the dark blue, the moon showing like a deep golden sun; heard all sounds—coyotes, wolves, howling and hollering at each other, smelt the warm steamy hides of elk and deer sniffing around, saw their dark shapes lined up beside the water's edge and vanish when I moved, their startled eyes glowing like small fires. All this told me I was alive, that it hadn't been a dream, the Sioux had been around.

Come morning when the grey dawn faded before the advancing sunlight creeping over the distant peaks, I moved into the shade.

My body burned with a fiery fever, the 'thing' no longer showed its baleful eye, buried in a bed of green yellowing flesh, a thin red line moving up my arm warning me I'd soon be dead.

Buzzards being patient, like Apaches, only had to wait, felt again their shadowy shapes hovering above, their sharp eyes knowing where I'd been and where I was now. If I didn't do something about it, once I got past reasoning

I'd just lay and die 'ere.

I eased off my boot, found a knife I kept stashed away back of my ankle bone, moved to the pool, my blurred vision and my voice muttering and groaning sent a hurrying through me and I recalled how it been years back, taking that English dude from Arizona to Abilene. Got himself a poisoned foot, had to stake him out and cut the rotting flesh away, damn near lost him. I held the knife, shaking and glinting in the early sunlight, held it against a rock, scraping it up and down till I had the notion it was real hot. Propped myself up in the muddy bank, my legs spread wide round a boulder, laid the 'thing' on it and cut deep into the pussy flesh. Writhing and screaming I leaned over the hot rock as the nail came out, bringing a small fleshy strip with it.

Can't recall how long I laid there, the sun being well up and over and clouds of flies buzzing in for a quick feast. The ugly pulpy mess told me it had to go, the pumping in my body crept to all corners, even my toes, behind my ears, top of my head, like it would soon blow off. In a few hours I wouldn't have any senses left. I laid the 'thing' in the water, cut deep, watched the slippery foul flesh float away, heard my groans like I'd swallowed sand and knew no more 'til them low-flying flapping buzzards wheeling about on the rocks told me I was still alive. I knew I had to keep cool, pulled handfuls of weeds and grass, thick with mud; got back into the shade, stashed the lot over my face and body and waited for what was to come.

A cool breeze drifted in from somewhere, felt it on the 'thing' like a soft touch. It was now a dripping fleshy ball, hanging on the end of a bloated arm. Heard Betsy's voice, 'Love you Tobe, call him Jamie, our son.' Saw Pa, scooping up a handful of dirt saying 'Smell it boy, ain't it sweet? Best Goddamn earth in this 'ere territory, where a man can put his roots down for his own kin.'

I hadn't ever smelt it, being as it was just dirt to me and I didn't have any feel for it as I'd walked behind the horses, watching 'em flick their tails at the flies. I'd dreamed of far off places, the Rockies, the river boats along the great Missouri, New Mexico, Serrie Mardie, the great railways snaking along into the vast unknown territory, mile-deep canyons, gorges, Texas Panhandle full to bursting with munching buffalo, great herds rumbling along the Chisholm Trail, the Goodnight Trail, Pikes Peak, Colorado, heaving prospectors scratching for silver and gold, wagon trains rolling along the wide prairies making for the Oregon, all the yearnings swelling up in my belly for a release from the plough. Used to ask myself why Pa hadn't gone with 'em; nope, he just had to hold that sweet-smelling earth. But it wasn't sweet, just hardbaked dirt, but his eyes were full of dreams, he couldn't see it.

Ma saying 'You're a good lad Tobe, just your pa wants you to grow up strong, got to be strong to survive, life's real hard for folks. Pa hasn't got a mean bone in his body, you just mind your pa and you'll be just like him.' And being a skinny little runt got the bad edge of all the bully boys, 'til I got the hang of it and when I saw satisfaction in his eyes, coming home without a black eye or a kick up the ass I knew I'd made it and just when we began to be real pards he got bushwhacked for a few dollars. Found him with a flyblown bloody hole in his back. All he got out of the harsh cruel land was a handful of dirt, a dream and a hole in his back.

Ma kinda gave up, faded away. I'm shaking, can't hear them buzzards. I'm no more'n thirteen years old, crying out, trembling, afraid, smelling the small hot room, the bedclothes, hearing her hard breathing and the coming death.

'Don't leave me Ma,' I'm crying, but she did, one hot afternoon and was buried next day beside Pa.

The few animals went somewhere, for a while folk fed me, but it soon faded away. I met up with Virgil, another orphan. We bummed around, sleeping rough, cleaning out slimy spittoons in the saloons, needed each other's bodies for warmth, grew hard, tough, able to

34

recognise the shysters, renegades, murderers and such. Drifted through Newton, Caldwell, Dodge City, Dallas, Hays, became trail hands, riding in the dust of the great herds.

Got ourselves a patch of land, a few cows, the beginning of the dream Pa had, but a greedy cattle baron and a two-timing sheriff playing both sides to middle burnt us out, killing Virgil, I high-tailing it out of that little Texas town leaving a dead sheriff's blood staining my land.

I'm choking, my throat's swelling up under my ears; I'm crying like I'm still a young'n, wearing my tattered jeans hanging off my body, like I'm wearing cast-off female's drawers. My brain is tumbling out these pictures; can see Virgil, both of us tall, rangey and bitter, had become men, needing like most the feel of the soft flesh of a clean upright female, waking up in the morning finding her beside you doing what had to be done, smell the sweet earth, bringing a contentment in our lives. I can't swallow the tears and spittle, maybe I'm dying on account I ain't never recalled it all so clearly before, these half-forgotten memories, rolling like shutters back of my eyes, that have been tucked away in my head. Why ain't they showed before, 'cause I don't want 'em now, don't want to recall time that far back when I had dreams and the Devil hadn't started sitting on my tail.

Can't feel the 'thing'. Is it still there, or have the coyotes eaten it? I'm floating light as a feather into nowhere. Is life only a dream and when I wake up I'll see Pa, holding a handful of sweet-smelling earth...

CHAPTER FIVE

I opened my eyes, my senses shoving them yesterdays away, my body taut and stretched with fever.

Had a notion I heard voices, ain't knowing on account my head wasn't acting up proper, but the fear of it, maybe redskins on the move, making for this waterhole, stirred my body into action.

I crawled and rolled, my head roaring like one of them iron belly puffers and edged into the close green away from the willows and cottonwoods, smelt the hot closeness of thick coarse grass and low bushes, near hollering as the 'thing' and my body caught itself on the sharp gravel, pebbles dried roots that clawed their way out of the earth like evil grasping fingers, my brain telling me I had to hide ... felt the wetness of torn flesh on my back and sides.

Suddenly I rolled down a slippery grade of loose broken rock and dried vegetation into a deep dark slit like a grave. The 'thing' caught onto a clump of half-rooted brush of spidery arms, spread out like a greedy animal; heard animal howlings from my guts and knew no more until the hot sun filtered through the green, spiking the sides, lighting up the gruesome hole. Slugs fat and slimy, worms, a few spiders, disturbed by my fall, moved slowly about.

My tongue and mouth stuck together, my empty belly no longer sending out a crying ache, reckon it was past caring.

The 'thing' an ugly red fleshy ball laying in the dirt, my swollen arm throbbed silently screaming, like it had become another 'thing'. I smelt the stink of it and my own sour rancid sweat, tasted the salty drips that trickled from my hairline. All the profanity I knew grunted out between my dry cracked blistered lips, felt 'em tear again.

The damp soil clung to my face and body and being grateful for the feel of it rolled my head into the dark corners and lay like an animal that had crawled away to die.

The sun must have near sunk over the western rims, dark shadows patterned the sides and the coolness of it lay over me like an invisible blanket, when my brain began to steady itself.

I heard my teeth chattering, felt my body having the shakes, heard voices, wheels rumbling, a dog barking, the sound of feet crunching through the dry leafy mould, twigs snapped, gravel moved, washing down into my hole, a dog's face with slavering dripping jaws, bared his teeth and looked over the edge. For a terrifying moment I had the notion it was for coming down onto me, then it made off with a spiteful yelp as a mouthful of profanity and a hard kick sent it on its way.

A coupla bearded faces, hidden under greasy leather slouch hats, peered down. 'Christ, it's a man!' said one, and before I knew it I was up and out, heard my groaning protesting body as the 'thing' dragged itself up with me.

They laid me beside the waterhole. I felt water being sloshed over me, into my mouth, I gulped at it, feeling it reach all corners, licked my blistered lips and tried to speak, my throat like it was filled with sand. I looked at the 'thing'. The dying sun reddened it, making it more fearsome.

I squinted at the faces bobbing about me, like they wasn't joined onto anything, leathery, stubbly, long bearded, small black eyes, like the 'thing' had held. Couldn't rightly make out what they was saying, just their showing broken yellow teeth.

Then all hell broke loose, they staked me out and between my howling and jerking, they cut away the remains of the pussy flesh, leaving a wet bloody shape showing fingers that moved

38

and writhed like it wanted to break free and bolt.

They rolled me up in a sweaty blanket, put me in the buckboard on deep sour smelling straw, the stench of it telling me flyblown bloody pelts and a pig had no doubt had the comfort of it before me.

Must have been moving most of the night, 'cause the sun was pinking when I opened my eyes.

I should have been dead, still racked with a sweaty fever and my bones rattled like there was no flesh on 'em. The sky looked mighty high up there, on account a gathering mountain of feathery clouds hung beneath it. Watching 'em told me I was getting my brains sorted out, on account I never ceased to be surprised at the changing moods above, 'cause there was always a vast ocean between the low clouds, the sun and the moon.

Yep, I was back in the land of the living, felt the cartwheels rumbling beneath my ass, heard voices. Still shaking, cushioned by the straw I rolled over and looked at the 'thing'. It lay, a red ball, with fingers sticking out of it, it glowed wet and shiny, covered in flies. My arm, swelled up to near twice its size, lay out of its torn sleeve.

I shuddered and groaned at the sight of it and asked myself where was I off to laying 'ere in my own shit and stink?

The wheels kept turning over bumps, into holes, sometimes only a couple of 'em tipping me sideways and the 'thing' pushing off the flies as it went with me.

Thankfully the wheels stopped, I made a harsh croaking sound as they clambered down and stared at me.

'The critter's alive, Seth,' said one. 'Sure looks like it Ezra,' said the other. They stood eyeing me like they'd just bought a pig.

Seth nodded. 'Reckon he's hungry.'

'No more'n a bag of bones,' added Ezra and put a mug of cold greasy soup to my mouth. The foul stuff went down, chunks of fat pork and beans with it. I gagged on it, but he held it firm.

'Reckon as how you're goin' to make it,' he said.

They had a good look at the 'thing', nodded to each other. 'You be goin't to make it stranger,' they both agreed, their small black eyes roaming over me. I smelt their stink and my guts sank near to my boots when I saw 'em more clearly. They was a coupla hill people, who spawned like rotting fungus away out in the vast wilderness like animals, shunning all decent civilization. Was said they was forgotten remnants of folk who'd fled from England and the cruelty that King James and his cronies had inflicted on 'em generations ago.

Was rumoured they'd grown half-witted

through breeding between themselves, but sly, cunning, scavenging about like coyotes, selling pelts, bear skins, mostly taking what they needed from unwary travelling folk who was unlucky enough to come up against 'em.

I'd met up with 'em, through the years, trading horses and such along the mining camps and lawless fledgling towns, a lost white tribe that no one wanted to know. Smelling 'em above my own stink my fuddled brain asked itself 'What the hell did they want with me, hadn't got a horse, no clothes to speak of, no damn nothing?' Their snakelike eyes, set well back in their boney faces, looked at me then each other. Close mouthed, they climbed back, got them horses moving and we was off.

I felt the world wobble about me as we bounced over rocky terrain, down through deep gullies, then gradually upwards.

Lost the scent of pines, oaks, rattled through an empty gorge, its sides pushing out the sun's fearsome heat that had been trapped in the scorching baking rock, and giant boulders with not enough air for the vultures and eagles to rise up on so they flapped screaming above us, their curved beaks pecking at nothing. Then we were out and climbing up through shelves of trees, more broken rockface, the pair of 'em champing on meat and taking long swallows of some kinda rotgut. Heard 'em belching and spitting and as the sun began to pale off making for the western rims, the wheels found more even ground. I smelt smoke, heard voices, barking dogs, squealing pigs and chickens. I became aware of booted feet, beating the dry cracked earth and a bunch of gawping faces lined along the edge of the buckboard.

Peering through my blistered eyeballs they didn't present a welcoming sight.

There they were, crowding in on each other, pushing and shoving. Tall, short, fat, thin, a few younger females. Stubble faced, long bearded old men, watery eyed and dribbling through their whiskers; old women like pale ghosts, all of 'em in a kinda sick silence, 'cause their dull eyes, sly, watchful, held something showing out of 'em I hadn't come across before. I began to think they was never going to move off, when a tall rawboned female came striding over.

What grey hair she had was pulled back and tied with string, about a foot of loose ends lay down her back, a grimy calico dress covered her long body. She eyed me out of light blue glassy eyes, their ringed pupils showing some excitement as she looked at the 'thing'. She nodded then, with a mighty shove, pushed 'em out of the way, picked me up like I was a young'n and made for one of them timbered shacks.

I heard myself groan as the 'thing' hit the dust, then I was in and laid on a bed. All the fighting in my body to stay alive sorta gave up, like I'd reached the end of it; felt myself sink into the mattress, like it was soft as down. The 'thing' lay beside me, I felt it close to my body.

It was as if my whole bag of skin and bone had telescoped together, that they no longer belonged to me. I was hovering outside of 'em as she dribbled some brew between my lips. I gulped at it greedily, heard it gurgling down into my belly. She became a tall shadow, inching up like a tree then faded away.

I was still hanging around in a half-knowing way 'cause I felt my stinking duds being pulled off, distant voices, like empty echoes in my brain, faces, lots of 'em with fleshy noses, open mouths, glassy eyed, nodding and leering, coming and going and still more of that brew trickled down my throat.

Sure was good; wasn't struggling against anything, couldn't figure out what they said 'cause I wasn't able to focus my eyes on 'em on account my head was a half-empty echoing ball.

Must have been a coupla days before my body became my own, the echoes gone, my ears picking up every sound—people, horses, pigs, chickens and my eyes picked out the thick timbered sides of the shack and another bed beside mine. A table fixed to the wooden floor, a window half-open, a large bearskin half-covered the floor.

I heard a movement, turned my head and saw

43

a gangling skinny young'n, about sixteen years old, sitting on the other bed.

He sure was a sorry sight, pale faced, dull eyed, long greasy hair hanging over his collar. His dirty feet hung out of tattered pants, showing about a foot of leg; his sweaty shirt hung off his body, the size of it, telling me it had once been used by some hefty critter.

He came over, pulled back the grimy blanket and looked at the 'thing', his long nails inching back the rag, eyeing the red fleshy ball. We both looked at it. The stinking flesh had gone and although it looked evil and red it no longer screamed at me and my arm had shrunk back to its bones, matching the other.

I saw the boney shape of my chest and ribs, near bursting out of my skin; hadn't got a belly, just an empty hole between 'em.

His eyes, deep and dark, shone with a kinda happiness as he touched my face, pulled the blanket back and went and sat on his bed.

I heard it rustle, no feathery clouds, mostly straw and none too fresh at that, each passing minute brought more awareness in me.

I tried to say 'Howdy' to him, all I got was a thick croak, but it got him moving, he was out that door quicker than a blue-assed fly.

After a few minutes he came back with that female who'd carted me in 'ere.

Towering over the bed she pulled back the blanket and looked at the 'thing'. Well satisfied she nodded and with one hefty pull had me half-up out of the bed, wedged against a coupla pillows, then went out.

I stared at the young'n, tasting my dried mouth and sticky lips.

'Water,' I managed, when the door opened and she came back with a bowl of hot meat, beans and grey bread. I went for it like a starving dog. 'You been right lucky stranger, ridin' this out,' she said. 'Some critter didn't like the cut of your jaw, sure had a mighty lotta hate, do that, sure had. Be a long time 'fore that hand be useful, don't reckon as how you be goin' to use a gun again.'

'I'm beholden to you ma'am,' I got out between mouthfuls of meat, addin' 'Don't reckon on staying around long, got to get my horse back and ...' I stopped, like I'd been poleaxed, my roan, my friend, and Bender, Ringer, what the bleeding hell was I doing 'ere. I pushed the bowl aside and figured on getting out of the bed. My skeleton of a body showed a sickening sight, the room swirled round.

'You ain't goin' nowhere, ain't fit for it. Been four days since Ezra brought you in,' she said.

'Four days, I been 'ere four days?' heard my voice getting back. She threw my duds on the bed, adding. 'You get into 'em, got all the time in the world, time ain't nothin out 'ere,' and she was gone.

The hot food sure had cleared my head. I

45

pulled on my duds, sat weakly on the bed, saw a cracked mirror and a face staring back at me. Long, gaunt, sunken eyes, beardless, ugly. I felt the tight skin over my cheekbones, some bastard had taken off my beard. I didn't know this critter, wasting four days in bed. I staggered to the window like an old man; a terrifying notion crept over me, a fear such as I'd never had before. My brain telling me I'd got to get myself well enough to shake this place off my back, felt my ice-cold vengeance taking over, had the shakes and it wasn't fever; it was hate. A silent howl went out of my body, but I heard it crashing against the timbered sides.

I looked at the 'thing'. Yep, it was my hand. The flesh was healing, drawing my palm tight into where the nail had been. I tried to curl my fingers over it, but they wasn't ready for it. I stretched 'em out but the pull was tearing the new flesh. I was sat on the bed staring at it, when they came in.

CHAPTER SIX

One by one they came over, a mighty strange bunch of critters.

'Name's Hope Larkin,' she said. 'Cyrus and Cabe, my sons, Abigail my daughter, old Ezra, great grandfather, Ezra grandfather, Ezra,

46

Benjamin and Ebeneza kin of 'em.' The last couple, around fifty years old, towered over the old bearded Ezra, their hard unblinking black eyes half-hidden under long unkempt hair and low brimmed greasy leather slouch hats.

They all sure was a right odd lot; old, dribbling, bleary eyed down to the young 'un sitting on the bed.

As an afterthought she turned saying, 'And him over there is Ben, he's kin only he don't talk, ain't spoke since he was a little young'n.'

I got kinda dizzy, they seemed to merge together from toothless, near toothless, the small black broken teeth of Cyrus and Cabe, for all they were only about thirty years old, to Abigail's yellowing uneven chewers. They was all smiling, sorta friendly, just it didn't reach their eyes, if you know what I mean, 'cause they showed a kinda shifty watchfulness that shouldn't have been there.

They all looked like they'd been hatched out of the same pod, wore their odd assortment of clothes as just a covering, not mindful of the fitting of 'em.

Abigail, nearing thirty years old, stood by the window, thin, boney, long straggly black hair hanging down her back, a grimy grey calico dress dragging on the floor, showing dirty feet, I reckon the rest of her being the same on account her face and neck sure looked in need of a splash of water.

Looking at 'em in this small hot dusty room, showing mouthfuls of grinning teeth and red gums, I had a flash of remembering. My brain slipped back to the last four days or more; wasn't a dream, they'd all been 'ere before, in my half-conscious state, looking me over.

'I'm right pleased to meet you all,' I got out.

'You be most welcome stranger, don't get folks comin' this far out,' said one. They all nodded.

Hope Larkin opened up. 'These are all my own folk. Come to think of it, we're all our own folk, keeps ourselves to ourselves, don't hold with the riotous livin', folks got out in them Devil's towns. Anyways we be over a hundred miles from any of that trash out there; ain't that right Ezra?'

One of 'em nodded, figure he was all of ninety years old, sticky eyed and dribbling. 'Devil's towns,' he mumbled, swaying like he was drunk as if the very force of speaking was toppling him over.

They all agreed and went out, Abigail stirring up the dust as she slowly left with 'em, her half-open mouth still showing them yellowing teeth.

Hope eyed me, well satisfied, saying, 'You just take it easy, ain't no hurry to be gettin' off, take a little time to put flesh back on your bones.' And she was gone.

I was left sorta stunned and with the sweaty

48

stink of 'em; don't reckon the oldsters had ever washed more'n once a year, if that.

But this bunch of harmless critters sure was doing me proud and I aimed to pay 'em back somehow before I left, sure did and told myself those old yarns about wild folk living out in the wilderness who'd come across the great oceans hundreds of years ago, was only a tale, dreamed up by half-drunk oldtimers, their bleary eyes set on another critter's half-empty bottle of rotgut.

I went to the window and peered out, sorta getting my bearings.

Wasn't exactly a meadow—holding several dozen strong timbered cabins—more a piece of land, dug out between the trees. Large gaps showed the pines had been stripped out, leaving rows of black stumps like rotting teeth, making way for the aspens, oaks, spruce, slewing down to cottonwoods and willows dangling their leaves in a swift-running creek.

A few cattle grazed, pigs and chickens rooted about, dogs curled up lazily in the shade, folk moved about doing their daily chores. All looked peaceful enough, half-dozing under the blazing sun; spied a few horses in a distant corral, a right pleasing sight.

Ben still sat, his dark eyes kinda watchful, yet they didn't show that certain something I couldn't put into words.

I went over to him. He drew back like he was

afraid.

I heard a voice shouting, 'Ben, where the hell are you?' and he went off.

I looked out of the window and saw Cyrus and Cabe shove him along to where the pigs were, then rode over to the wild bucking horses.

I felt the sun's heat blasting the roof of the cabin, began to get the dismals again, like it came in waves, drifting through my brain. Wasn't dead, my belly full, a bed to lay on, kindly folk, as the minutes ticked by I recalled my horse, sure was a noble mount. The tearing pain of it all, my guts just wasn't taking it no how, the knowing of another Goddamn bastard riding him. It's when I get them lonely times I need him, the warm smell of him, his soft velvety mouth, the sounds he makes just for me, knowing he's standing by, always waiting; my whole body screams as I sit recalling it all. Out there is a vast green ocean, spreading out in the distance, covering the rims, and I'm drowning in it. Don't know where the hell I am, and too damn weak to find out. I ain't reasoning right, 'cause my brain slides about. I put my head between my knees, ain't ashamed to say I tasted the salt from my wet dripping eyes.

I let the sweet tasting brew from the bottle on the table wet my mouth, ain't got a bite to it, but sure is kinda pleasant.

Must have been a coupla hours later when Abigail came in with a plate of jack rabbit, beans, bread and coffee. I'd shook off the dismals, got quite perky. She sat on the chair, watching me eat. 'I cooked it,' she said, her eyes shining, a right pleased expression on her face.

I nodded. 'Real good Abigail.' And it was, holding the carcass in my good hand, pulling the meat from the bones with my teeth.

She'd tied her lanky hair back, making her small face more birdlike and narrow, her deepset dark eyes more alive. I felt 'em roaming over me. She quickened her breathing, her skinny body moved under her dress, she touched my hand, with her small clawlike fingers. 'It's gettin' better Mr...?'

'Tobe Harris,' I gave her.

'Tobe Harris.' She repeated it a coupla times and it struck me Hope hadn't asked me who I was, where I was making for. Abigail piled the plates up and left.

I was being fed and watered like a prize animal, hadn't ventured out of the cabin, 'cause I sure was a sorry sight, but each day the meat came back onto my bones, had a right good feeling about the place. Cyrus, Cabe and a few others passed the time of day, I felt like a pig being fattened up for a Saturday shindig. Hope called me Tobe and Abigail became Abby, yet I couldn't pull myself together. Had always been

51

a hell-raiser, mean, ornery, killed more ornery critters than I can recall and my dull eyes stared accusingly back from the flyblown dusty mirror. 'Reckon I'll soon be pushing off,' I said to Abby after polishing off another heap of chunky meat. My whiskers were coming back, felt nearly as good as new.

She shrugged. 'Ain't strong enough, ain't no hurry; reckon Ma, Cyrus and Cabe could do with a little help out there,' she muttered and went off.

Ben showed up, smelling more like them black legged pigs than that pile of rotting garbage out in a deep pit between the trees he'd been busy on.

'I'm Tobe,' I said. 'Feeling right fine, even my hand shows more like it used to be.'

His white face twitched like he'd been bitten by a hornet, stretching it sideways, showing strong even teeth, as he tried to speak.

His bony arms came out of his scruffy shirt like a coupla spare ribs that had broken through, hanging loose.

It was his eyes that got at me, sad, that said much more than his moving mouth. I figured the poor critter was real troubled, his nerves stretched tighter than them polecats' guts hanging out on a pole.

He pulled something out of his pocket, a hard lump of greasy fat, laid it in my hand, working it into the dry middle, round and round, easing my fingers over. It felt real good. I caught on, patted his shoulder. Hearing footsteps he shoved it into my pocket and went out.

Hope came in. 'Reckon you be able to get out a bit,' she said 'bein' as it's Sunday. Folks 'ere don't reckon on doin' many chores, bein' as it's the Lord's day. Always keep Sunday for the Lord.'

Her long angular shape blocked the doorway. I spied Abby hovering about listening. I kept the lump of fat hidden. I reckon it was then I began to have a nasty feeling about the place; couldn't find a reason, just it was there and growing.

CHAPTER SEVEN

Stepping out into the Lord's day sure was something. Squinting against the sun's glare, hitting me like an iron rod, I spied folk standing round a roasting pig.

Abby and a coupla females passed by laughing, showing their soon-to-be-rotten teeth. Sunday wasn't a day for the washing of bodies on account Abby still wore the same sweat she'd had all the week. I made my way through the aspens and cut down pines along a narrow track leading to a corral.

Cyrus and Cabe busy with horse breaking, their grey check shirts sticky with sweat clinging to their bodies as they dodged about in the swirling dust and screaming bolt eyed horses.

I shouted over all friendly like, 'You got a spare one?'

Dusting themselves off, they came over. 'Ain't got none,' said Cyrus, spitting from a dust-caked face. Cabe eyed me from red rimmed watery eyes blinking at the dust settling in 'em. 'Just tellin' him we ain't got no spare horses,' added Cyrus.

Cabe nodded. 'That's right, ain't got none.'

I bristled a mite 'What about them, ain't buzzards?'

'Just heard right,' said Cabe. 'We ain't got none.'

They stood leering at some secret joke, their stubbly faces dripping with sweat that spread in black widening patches through their shirts.

I held myself in check, saying, 'Being as how my horse and gear being stole, I need a mount, I'll see you get paid when I reach Denver.'

I was talking to nothing, they just up and rode off.

I turned to walk back, saw Hope, Abby and a few others watching. They moved off when I reached the cabin.

My guts a tight hard ball, instinctively my hand reached for my gunbelt, it wasn't there;

54

hadn't ever felt so naked, so alone, no horse, no gun.

I sat on the wooden step, Ben showed. 'Where is this place?' I asked. He shook his head.

'You ever been out of it?' I probed.

No, he hadn't and pointed at Cyrus, Cabe and a few others and nodded, they had. At last the pig was ready, I watched 'em cutting it up, shoving great chunks of it down their throats. Then it struck me; wasn't no young'ns, no yelling babies.

Ben was the youngest critter here.

One of 'em started playing a fiddle, sending cat calls like a dying animal. Mugs of rotgut got swilled down from a barrel rolled down through the pines, past a solitary cabin perched up a steep grade.

Wasn't hard potent brew, but sure got 'em all going, dancing and jugging about kicking up the dust, shaking it off their long bony faces and out of their deepset eyes and open mouths.

Sure sign they was enjoying their Lord's day. Soon they had enough and wandered off into the shade to sleep it off, leaving the half-eaten carcass to hordes of blue assed flies and again it hit me, the menfolk was damn near all Ezras, Ebenezas, Cabes, Cyruses and a few odd ones in between.

Come evening when the sun began to make for them western rims, wherever they might be,

Hope, Abby and a coupla old Ezras came and chatted, telling me how well I looked, 'yes the hand was healing right fast'. Abby sat on the wide step, her legs spread out, her feet scuffling the dust. Hope nudged her saying, 'You just keep your knees together Abby, shame on you, sittin' there with no drawers on, when we got ...' she hesitated, searching her brains for the right word.

'Company, ma!' shouted Abby, putting her legs down, just her dirty feet poking out from the hem of her grimy dress. She grinned, showing her small ratlike teeth, smoothing the sweaty calico dress, her clawlike hand moving over it like a tethered animal, scraping, pinching tucks into it, a silly kinda smile, sly and cunning showing on her face. They all looked at each other, nodding, knowing each other's thoughts.

'Seems you want a horse,' said Hope. 'Reckon as how we ain't got none; shouldn't be worryin' Cyrus and Cabe, 'cause they be takin' 'em to the minin' camps, those Devil's places. Be gone in a few weeks.'

'There's other horses,' I argued.

'That's as maybe,' she retorted, 'ain't got no spare horses, as Cyrus and Cabe said; best leave it be.'

My skin crawled, damn near lifting off my flesh, something sick and terrifying was all about me, I could taste it on my lips, feel it.

56

She passed a bottle of brew round, same as I'd had before. I drank the dark liquid with the rest of 'em and right pleasing it was.

The evening faded into night quickly, as it does in these 'ere parts. I forgot my early misgivings, felt right good and went in as the moon showed a faint slither of silver in a dark blue sky.

Spent some time greasing my hand, my head all mixed up, lay sorta half-asleep, heard soft footfalls, spied Benjamin and Ebeneza creep in and take Ben out, half an hour later he came back and lay trembling under the blanket. I went over, his tormented eyes told me what had happened. Sick to my guts I went back to bed, had another drink and sorta half-drifted off into nowhere.

Later I heard the door open, Abby and another female came in. I felt Abby's clawing hand on my shoulder, her fingers moving over my flesh, my hair. The other touched me; Abby turned like wildcat, clawing her face. Through half-open eyes I saw 'em glaring at each other like a coupla fighting whores in a cat-house.

'He's mine,' whispered Abby.

'Maybe he won't want you,' sneered the other, a thin trickle of blood running down her face.

'He's mine, just you remember it, else you just might have an accident. Won't be the first,' threatened Abby.

57

They left. I lay half-asleep in a kinda living nightmare till dawn showed itself. Restless, Ben came over, looked at the bottle, tried to tell me something, gave up and went out.

I washed and was for going outside when he came back, put something in my hand and pointed to the bottle.

My brain nearly exploded in a kinda terror at what had been happening to me, breaking down my resistance. So in the end I'd be what, no bloody nothing.

It was Peyote, a spineless cactus button, growing just above the ground, doesn't grow much north of the Mexican border. How the hell had it got 'ere?

Chewed or made into a drink it made a critter right happy, even to having delusions; it was reckoned by some Indian tribes it would cure their sickness, more likely kill 'em.

Was no wonder I drifted about in a kinda lost way, 'cause my brain was being pickled, else my mean and ornery nature would have made me feel like a bull with a bolt of lightning up his ass.

I had to keep cool, stone cold, have patience and I ain't a patient critter; just play 'em along 'till I felt strong enough and time was right to make a run for it.

'Ben,' I said, 'think on this, there's your world out there, I aim to make it and you're going with me, like them birds, beaking away up in the blue.' His eyes followed 'em and a wet trickle slid down his face. My guts knotted up at seeing it.

I no longer drank the brew, just slowly drained it away and always the bottle was filled up.

Got to know Abby, was times when she spoke quite rational, others when she became childlike, vacant, as if she were two people in one skin, the stronger one always fighting for control and never quite making it.

Like the rest of the women she'd giggle, snigger and always her face showing the same sly cunning.

She'd slide her long nails over my arm, press hard and let go, her dull eyes held a sudden gleam at her inner thoughts.

A coupla more weeks passed. I'd walk through the trees and brush so thick the sun found it hard to sprinkle through, saw a burial ground, thick with humps and lumps and grass growing in between and always some of 'em would be there, I'd hear 'em and then their stubbly faces would be showing their deepset black eyes watchful and their cursed smiling faces. I'd play along with 'em, grinning. Had a curiosity about the cabin, more so when I spied Hope footing it over with a bowl of hot food, asked Ben, he just shied off, a look of fright stretching over his already twitching face.

One morning as the grey fingers of dawn

pushed away the night I went outside. All was quiet, like a dead place, not even a dog, pig or chicken broke the silence.

I felt right good, getting my meat back on my bones, my brains wasn't swimming about, my hand no way ready to handle a gun, but being as I'm a two-gun man and handy with a knife I'd given much thought on hightailing it out of this hellhole, taking Ben with me. He'd do real fine working along them mining camps, kinda find himself. Hadn't set eyes on a trail yet, on account them bastards was always showing up when I did my roaming.

All this was well up in front of my mind when I slid off to take a peek at the cabin.

Was peopled, on account a light showed in the window night times and Hope wouldn't be taking food and coffee to anything other than a two-legged critter. A long drawn out blood curdling howl splintered the silence, getting the drowsy pigs, dogs, chickens opening up all over and birds shaking the tree tops.

Wasn't an animal, reckon my skin moved an inch, felt the hairs on my neck stand up stiff as the bristles on a hog's back, saw a hairy hand drag itself over the window, the timbers shake.

'You best see it, won't be satisfied 'til you do.' Hope stood there, a bucket in one hand, a pitchfork in the other.

Her face set grim and hard, a look of resignation as to what was inside showing from her unblinking blue eyes.

CHAPTER EIGHT

She opened the heavy timber door. The shadowy room showed a critter more like an animal than a man—crouched in the corner, head sunk onto wide shoulders, his long grey hair lay over his back like a shawl. His large eyes like boiled eggs stared from deepset sockets, like the rest of the other folk hereabouts. His long arms stretched out, the wide hands groped and clawed like a grizzly bear. His lips curling back from black broken teeth were bared like a cornered animal.

He leapt forward, dragging at the short chain, causing him to crash onto the floor, his long-nailed fingers spreading, reaching, hands outstretched, his mouth opening and shutting.

She shoved the food across with the pitchfork. Like an animal he launched himself onto it, his slobbering mouth sloshing over it, licking, snarling. Suddenly, as if part of his brain still worked, he lifted his head and butted it against the pitchfork, knocking Hope sideways. She wasn't ready and slipped on the greasy floor, his long arms struggling to reach the fork. She gave a scream, I pulled her back, grabbed the fork and edged towards the door.

Still snarling, he half-stood up, greasy meat and gravy hanging off his beard, his long fingers searching for it and shoving it into his mouth.

Hope scrambled to her feet in no way terrified at this gruesome sight.

'You just ain't your usual self Ezra, you just ain't,' she grumbled and turning to me she added, 'And what you be doin' 'ere, this be family business, no call to be nosin' around, still, reckon as I'm grateful to you, he'll have hold of me one day, won't be good for him if he does on account I keep him alive, Cyrus and Cabe well, that's another matter, don't reckon they'll bother with him.'

He'd quietened a mite, she sloshed water over the floor, sweeping away the filth with a hard broom in one hand, the pitchfork in the other.

The early sun crept in, showing up his half-naked body, covered only in filthy rags. 'Reckon as he'll have to be done,' she said, 'take more'n a coupla days to get him quiet, got some brew ready, nearly gets him half-asleep and laughing, make it powerful strong, put some more clothes on him; 'course he's real powerful, takes more'n a dozen of us sometimes, don't reckon on doin' him more'n a coupla times a year.'

She shut the door, winding the thick chain across it. 'Real powerful, broke many a chain, just hope one day I'll find him dead. God rest

62

his soul, best for all of us, he's round seventy and still mighty strong. Reckon that madness feeds him, sometimes he's different, knows he's a man, got a man's needs, more's the pity and he's right artful; thinks, plans, stands up best he can peerin' out of the window, moves along followin' the sun, like he wants to feel it and the moon, just the once he kept a platter—forced it between the timbers, tryin' to pull 'em apart, caught him just in time. Like I say, he thinks, can't take no chances.'

I was right glad to be out in the fresh air, smell the pines, the earthy moisture not yet taken up by the rising sun's fearsome heat; saw the sparkling creek flashing along between the green, the cabins hugging the ground, some like brown nuts amongst the grass in the distance, a right pretty place.

Saw a great elk, head held high, sniffing the distance between us, bringing a kinda sanity, this beast in its complete innocence having nothing of man's evil ways. Didn't belong 'ere, was wild and free to roam and nibble the fast-growing early grasses, drink from the creeks, rivers. Just to see it brought home to me I'd got to go, there was another world out there.

Hope sat on a log, her hard face crumpled into a sorta silent grief saying, 'He's kin, my brother, been in there nigh on sixteen years, misbehaved himself in the eyes of the Lord, right sinful, Old Ezra and Old Ebeneza the

Elders, held council and he was turned out. Hung about for months, out in the wild, crawled back one day, starvin', gored all over like he'd been trampled by a mad steer, covered in blood. We reckoned it was God's will, the Lord speakin' from the wilderness sayin' "we should take him back". He was near ravin', we tied him to a log, right terrified he was at the sight of water, foamin' at the mouth; we reckoned a rabid skunk or mad dog had got at him and he had bear claw marks on his back. We built the cabin and he's been in there ever since.

'Wasn't what the Lord had in mind to kill him, guess he wanted us to forgive, so there he is.

'Young Ben, he's been in there enough times to know he don't like it. Old Ezra put him there for a sorta punishment when he was small, he never spoke since.'

The cabin shook, heard the chains rattle. 'Tis God's will, this be our land, God's given land and 'ere we stay, yes God's given land.' She sat, lost in herself, it was like that ruckus in there had loosened some dim parts of her mind, sliding back to their early times when their forefathers had searched for peace and solitude from their own land and that old king who sure had been after their hides.

She went on 'Don't misbehave on Sundays, praise the Lord. Benjamin and Ebeneza they

64

don't misbehave on Sundays, they find it hard to heed the Lord's teachin's, havin' no womenfolk of their own, got man's needs.' She stopped a moment then added, 'Abby she be a right fine girl, pure minded is Abby.' Then, like a kinda threat, she added, 'There's bears, cougars, wolves out there, real close they are, even dig them graves up. You get yourself lost, you be a dead man, have had folks up 'ere before, they shoved off, never came back, one hung himself in that tumbledown shack over by the garbage pit, seems he couldn't settle. Cyrus and Cabe brought him in, turned out he was a preacher, reckoned he could tell us about the Lord—we hoped he'd settle down with young Faith, but he got scared and took off, Benjamin and Ebeneza brought him back, near starved to death, reckon his Lord never came up to his expectations, found him hangin' one morning. Like I said, ain't wise to wander out there.'

I felt her glassy blue eyes on me as I said, 'I best be off.' Her grey hair hanging down her back, filth and water dripping from her leather skirt, a confident smirk on her face, like that clearing up that floor wasn't the only early morning chore she'd done. I felt my ticker pounding, my blood roaring through my veins, had never felt so afeared before, not the Apache, pressing a burning brand against my face, the Cheyenne roasting my feet, even Bender and Ringer's torturing ways, 'cause out 'ere such happenings are a way of life, had put such fear into me.

It's like I'm caught in a web, its sticky threads binding me tight, I dream of smiling faces, leering faces, silent mouthings and the sweet scented nights that sucks at my guts; come morning I wonder if I still got 'em and my skin starts crawling again, knowing I'm trapped in a sorta living sore, hidden away behind deep forest and mountainous rocky terrain. My hand gripped and stretched, I felt the lump of fat rolling about inside it. I feel in my bones the time is coming for me to go; my muscles are hardening, like rope, pushing and straining.

She turned, breaking into my thoughts, smiling, I smiled back, she gave a kinda satisfied nod and went on her way.

I met Ben, making for the garbage pit. He beckoned me to follow, I near gagged at the stench of it.

He bent down, feeling around, then came up with a pig's bladder, opened it and pulled out the small gun and thin knife I'd carried in my boots, tucked away back of my ankle bone.

'Christ Ben, Oh Christ,' I choked, just ain't no words for it. Ain't ever going to be, he looked right pleased with himself. I gripped his hand, pointed to the sky, 'When it rains we'll be off, leave no tracks,' I said. He nodded and stashed the bladder away. The place was singing, the trees, birds, the waving grasses, the creek, or was it my head? I felt alive and bursting, the dismals had vanished . . . even the foul stink had a kinda sweet smell to it.

Abby came shouting over. 'Ma says as how you take breakfast with us.'

I swear I heard the Devil laughing as I footed it along to the cabin; reckon he couldn't wait to get out of this 'Lord's' place.

CHAPTER NINE

Their cabin, strong timbered like the rest of 'em, had the usual heavy shuttered window, chunky sods of earth laying under the thick timbers that spanned the roof top, sprouted grass, even a few early blossoms. It had a coupla chimneys, several rooms spread out from the near side and rear; back of it chickens pecked and black legged pigs rooted about. A real family place, holding upright God fearing, peaceful folk, it even smelt peaceful when I went in, smelling the strong odour of bacon, eggs and coffee wafting out all over.

The peaceful look still showing inside, the main room about twenty feet by eighteen, a large open fireplace edged back into a neat stone pile, holding sparkling logs, high backed wooden chairs lined along a narrow table, through the middle of the room. The floor had a scattering of cougar skins, bearskins and sacking rugs. An old wooden rocking chair—the seat long gone— now filled with straw and feather cushions, near touching the floor, stood in the corner. An old woman sat in it, not moving, stiff, like she was dead.

Her white wrinkled face showing skin so loose it hung off the bones like pieces of faded papers. Her lips were pushed forward, wet and dribbling, small bubbles eased out of the sides as she just about breathed.

Long white tangled hair straggled over her shoulders, her knuckles showed white under the straining skin of her hands, clasped tight in her lap.

Hope went over shouting, 'This be the stranger Ma, he's right well now, just needs feedin' up.'

The old woman jerked back to life, sucking back the spittle, a pair of faded blue eyes settled on me as she leaned forward nodding. 'Hope, she told me about you, should be dead, all should be dead.'

'Now Ma,' said Hope, 'don't you go wanderin' off.'

'What's that you say?' wheezed the old woman irritably. 'Ain't no call to shout. This be the man Abby reckons on settlin' down with, you told me about.' Her eyes brightened. 'How's that then, gettin' them hands on some female flesh? Ain't much of it 'ere abouts, them females out there ain't no good for breedin'.'

Her eyes became dull again, as she wandered off, her hands plucking at the blanket. 'You be that stranger Seth and Ezra brought in, Hope told me about it, why ain't I seen you before, where's Abby, that damn fool gal ain't old enough to see to that young'n, I'm cold, should be dead, all should be dead.'

Hope butted in, bristling a mite. 'Now Ma, you just sit quiet and Abby will get your meal,' turning to me she added, 'she don't know what she's sayin', turned ninety-five years old, gets all muddled up does Ma, Faith that's her name, but she don't remember it now.'

'Faith's my name,' came back the wheezing voice 'ain't in no muddle, do recall who I am, where's Abby and that dratted young'n?'

'Here,' said Abby, giving her a plate of soup and bread.

'Don't get no sense out of old Faith any more, right stubborn she is, won't let no one only Abby tend to her, reckon she'll have to put up with me when Abby gets settled,' said Hope. She turned as Ben, Cyrus and Cabe came striding in, 'You just all set to and eat.'

I sensed that she was boss to 'em all, telling 'em about the pigs, chickens, pelts and horses, traps and snares, to be looked at, as the great mounds of food went down our throats.

I was knowing of the hard black eyes of Cyrus and Cabe, settling on me more times than

I liked and the way they dug their knives into the thick meat gave me the notion it was a kinda warning.

The old woman sat like she was dead once more. All our bellies filled, I made a move to go.

'Ain't no need to be hurrying off,' said Hope, 'you and young Ben best go searching for them traps and snares along the creek.'

Cyrus and Cabe sat easy, grease hanging onto their stubbly faces, on account they ate like pigs and smelt like 'em. Their legs spread out under the table, gunbelts holding dusty guns, tight under their bellies.

Feeling right ornery at the sight of 'em I said, 'You letting me have one of them horses, can't get far without one?'

Cabe bared his teeth. 'Told you before, ain't got no spare horses.' A nasty atmosphere filled the room, Ben fidgeted about like he'd got a burr on his ass. 'We be right pleased for you to stay over a while,' said Hope, 'reckon as how you owe us on account you was near dead when they fetched you in.' Again I felt a threat in the sudden silence.

'Reckon I do at that,' I gave 'em, all easy, grinning. 'I figure about a month, then I'll be off back to Wyoming, got my kin back there.' Hope snorted, rattling the plates, showing them long teeth.

'Don't figure your kin amount to much, you

bein' so far away, no house, no guns, no nothin', near dead and someone hatin' your guts enough to shove a rusty nail through your hand. You best stay awhile, ain't no way out for a critter on foot, there's deep canyons, dried out creeks, empty riverbeds, is a river about forty miles east, flowin' into a deep gorge, don't know where it goes or where it comes from. Cyrus and Cabe and a few other menfolk knows the way out of 'ere.'

A silence came over like a deafening thunderclap. I wasn't going anywhere and they all damn well knew it, same as the rest of 'em outside.

I looked at 'em and their half-smiling faces, God-fearing folk who listened to the voice of the Lord in the wilderness. Abby waited to be bedded, her belly swelling out with my seed growing in it, on account this lost white tribe were dyin' off one by one, their bodies carrying no fertile seeds, taking another last desperate chance to keep together, multiply, their brains steeped in happy drink.

I looked at Ben, sixteen years old, no young'ns running about and felt a growing hate of 'em settle in me, smiled back and at Abby clearing away the dishes, fanning out her sour sweat, half-grinning, a growing excitement showing in her flushed face.

Hope setting well back, her long lean face looking right satisfied, her lips pursed together, the glassy blue eyes on both of us as if it had all been decided.

Cabe and Cyrus, belching and spitting, their faces also having that same satisfied look.

The old woman proving what she'd already said, sniggered and rocked in the chair, just the top of her head showing. 'Ain't goin' nowhere stranger, folks always stay 'ere in the end, ain't no way out, you see, no way out, should be dead, all be dead ... where's Abby?'

'Shut that dribblin' old fool up ma,' shouted Cyrus. 'The old coot should be dead, reckon as how I'll do it.'

Hope lost her satisfied smug smile. 'You just mind your mouth. When the Lord's ready he'll take her, like he takes all of us.'

'Yeah Ma,' Cyrus caved in like a young'n and he followed Cabe out. I senses the evil in 'em hadn't been quashed, just they'd got enough sense not to show it. I reckon they could hardly wait to shake the dust of the place off their feet, get down to them fledgling towns, mining camps, boozing and whoring and wasn't blaming 'em any.

CHAPTER TEN

I went with Ben along the creek's edge, the sun sending down an early promise of what was to come on account the early dew had already been sucked up and a few lizards were spreading themselves on the rocks. We found the bloated carcasses of beavers and jack rabbits, a coyote, their open mouths silently screaming, their glazed eyes still holding the knowing of their coming death.

Ben led me into close thicket, pulled a log from a hole and fetched a grey and red check kerchief. It was mine; he shook out a shower of dollars. He sure was full of surprises, been right artful to filch 'em from under their noses when I was brought in.

There it was, the signed note for a thousand dollars for the sheriff of Denver and my three hundred dollars, sure showed he had something in mind. He sat back on his heels grinning.

'You're a real fine lad Ben, real fine,' I said and reckoned whilst I didn't hold a good card hand I'd got my reasoning back, meat growing over my bones, maybe there was five aces in a pack. We made camp, grinning at each other as we ate and drank coffee.

About an hour after midday we hid our findings back in the hole and made our way back, the running water got sorta slow, as if that burning orb up high had stunned all life into silence. Not even a bee buzzed, just the heat rising from the ground forming a blue haze in the distance—saw no leering faces, watching, to their thinking I'd got my watchdog with me.

I smelt my own sweaty stink, near strong as the bloody flyblown pelts. We kept moving, figured I'd spied some of 'em stalking us like dark shadows between the trees, nudged Ben. He walked on, not a glance, but he knew, saw his jaws twitch, wasn't fear, reckoned he was grinning and it crossed my mind he hadn't had the twitches so much the last few days and was not so Goddamned hangdog. Reckon he had all the makings of being a fine lad, once he got away.

Saw the settlement lining up before us as we made our way through the cottonwoods and willows.

He went off with the skins. I sat by the water's edge, it had been real good, hadn't felt smothered by the evil presence of these sick minded half-witted 'Lord's' people.

Then up in front of my mind came Bender, Ringer, my horse, the searing burning vengeance, a raw tearin' pain that clawed at my guts like an extra living thing had burned into me, bent me over. I felt my hand gripping the wood in my fingers getting the feel of it, stretching, straining, sure was satisfying. I'd made a coupla small leather bags, filled 'em with sand and pebbles, tight as stones, fixed 'em to a thin strip of leather. A deadly silent weapon I'd learnt from Dog-face, a halfbreed Sioux, an army scout.

I saw my face reflected in the water, ugly,

stubbly and mean. A terrible look in the eyes, staring back; was like I was seeing the Devil, 'cause that was him leering at me.

It went like a flash when I heard Abby footing through the grass. She sat down, again I smelt her stale unwashed body, her unkempt greasy hair, her small bony face. 'Ma says as how you can help Benjamin and Ebeneza whilst Cyrus and Cabe be gone,' she said. 'Ain't it nice you got real well now, sure was a sorry sight when Seth and Ezra brought you in?' Her hand held tight on my arm, her fingers kneading into my flesh, her face flushed, the dark deepset eyes bright.

'I like it 'ere, just the two of us,' she added, 'and Ben has got a real feeling for you, reckon as how you'll settle down real well not like ...' She stopped, got sorta lost then went on. 'This be our land, Ma says as how the Lord guided our folk over 'ere long years ago. Old Ezra and Ebeneza used to tell me tales of how it was, but they been dead well over twenty years and they got all that from their kin.'

She gave a little giggle. 'Ain't it kinda funny, all these Ezras, Cabes, Ebenezas? Did have some Jacobs and Elis but they died off. Like we're all brothers and sisters, yet we can't, can we Tobe? I look at 'em all sometimes and can't recall when I ever set eyes on any other than them.' Again she hesitated—'Well only a few times and they ...' She got up, walked along the water's edge, her feet pushing through the mud saying, 'Old, Old Ezra used to say be a good child, the Lord will look after you and all of us. But lots of women died having babies, all blue they was and didn't breathe, old Faith said as how it was their fault, lettin' the Devil in, so the Lord took 'em as well, ain't none been born since young Ben.' She looked kinda cunning, like she held a close secret. 'I know I ain't got the Devil in me. I knows.'

She kicked up the mud, laughing, some of it settled back on her face, in her hair, young Faith came along, both of 'em played like children, laughing at nothing, splashing in the mud, yet they was aware of me, a man, watching, as they giggled and whispered, eyes sharp and sly. I spied Hope watching as they moved off and felt sick to my guts. The muddled old woman was right. *Should all be dead.*

I went to our cabin, washing off the day's sweat, drained away some of the brew from the bottle.

Cooking smells lay close and steamy, the stifling heat sweating me out before I'd hardly got my arms into a clean shirt. Grinned to myself at the notion it must have covered a right meaty critter 'cause I reckon it would have fitted real snug over one of the snuffling black hogs. My hands suddenly took a dislike to it, dropping away like it had burrs tangled in it, as

I recalled the tales drooling out of the mouths of drifting drunken bums, old trappers and such as to how these scavengers went out pillaging and killing, sure knew what they was saying. Some poor bastard had laid and breathed in it, but I guess he wouldn't take offence at me wearing it and pushed the thoughts away as I covered my ass with it and went outside.

Bunches of critters were making for the lonely cabin, its timbers heaving and straining. A deep-throated howl slowly rang out. I felt it touch my skin, the bristles rise on my neck. That poor mad bastard sure paid a terrible price for his misbehaving. Suddenly the door burst open and there he was, squinting at the glaring sunlight, swaying on his bent legs, the broken chains dangling off his body. He eyed the curious crowd moving in on him, then held out his hands, went down on his knees, grovelling in the dust, choking sounds like long-forgotten words dragged themselves out of his mouth.

Cabe, Cyrus, Benjamin and Hope walked over with a rope and the pitchfork. He stood up best he could, long strings of spittle threading their way through his long beard. Blood dripped from his ankles where the chains had cut deep, his shoulders shook, then all of him. He looked at the sky, the green forests and them, and he was hogtied like a steer ready for branding, I saw a flicker of intelligence in his eyes and a sorta terrible sadness cross his face as he was dragged back in and my guts ached for the poor demented critter who wanted to be dead.

Folk drifted off as they came out, closing the door on the shaking cabin. I made my way back, heard a voice in our cabin. It was Abby saying, 'Please Lord, douse the fiery want he's got in him to leave us all, before it burns him up and he makes off into the wilderness, 'cause I fear for him Lord.' She stopped on hearing me. 'Food is ready,' she said and went.

We all ate kinda quiet, lost for words, just the sound of eating, drinking and the old woman's slobbering in the corner. Maybe it was the heat, hanging thick like a sticky blanket, no air came over from the distant green rims, no vultures tangled up in the sky, even the tall grasses and willows were still and the great red ball hung up high, sending down its fiery blast, the sky taking on the colour of a belly puffer's molten innards.

As the day wore on it gave way to distant humps of greying clouds, forming into vast mountains, taking over the red. Heard a faint rumble, like a huge growling animal was crunching up the rocky gorges hidden behind the deep forests. I gazed at the moving mass, which told me there sure was a wet and windy sky lining way over the mesa. My ticker raced, a great surge of life swept over me. It was time.

No one took any notice of Ben, the pig's

bladder surfaced, my kerchief, meat and bread found its way into the cabin, a coupla slickers hung on a nail and we waited for that great monster to move over, wash the place away and us with it.

Cabe showed, as the threatening sky turned more black. 'Going to be a hell of a storm when it breaks, you and Ben best look to the cattle whilst we look to the horses,' he said and was gone. But it didn't break, just blotted out the sun. The great mass hung low over the tree top, the ground rumbled beneath our feet. Sweat ran off of us like we'd been ducked in a water trough. It was like night had taken over day. Then, out of the eerie silence, came a flash of lightning; like a giant lizard darting across the sky, it stood, legs spread wide, its tongue forking out, lashing and darting into the ground.

A huge clap of thunder stung our ears as a thunderbolt hit between the trees. Then all hell let loose, the great lumbering animal breathed all over the settlement. Like matchsticks trees fell, their roots but clawing fingers reaching for nothing. Thunder ripped the sky apart, lightning showed up layers of cloud waiting to burst open. Then, like a giant broom, the wind came howling across, sweeping all before it—great trees bent and swayed, their thick branches tangling and broken, sucked up by the fearsome force of it. Heard the pounding hooves of cattle and horses as they broke free, racing away in the deep black, heard critters shouting above it all, as we edged out.

CHAPTER ELEVEN

I made for the burial ground, on account no trees stood in it, told Ben to stay close else I'd lose him; still no rain, these dry storms being more dangerous . . . seems they got a real mean punch in 'em, right eerie.

Must have been a coupla hours before the rains came and we was deep in the forest of howling demons smashing themselves against the trees with a deafening roar like an army of locusts had been blasted from the trees, hitting the ground like bullets, hailstones big as birds' eggs lay like early winter on the ground, crunching beneath our feet as we inched our way through gullies, ditches, uprooted low bushes and trees, cluttered debris. Listened to the branches untangling themselves from each other, cracking and straining treetrunks trying to push themselves back in the ground; scrambled through bushes, loose rockfall, upturned slippery boulders and clumps of moss.

Must have been a coupla hours before midnight the sky still showing black and menacing. I didn't reckon any of 'em would figure I'd be foolhardy enough to make off this way into nowhere. Might even tell themselves I'd been killed, which gave us time before they missed Ben. Had the notion they'd figure we'd gone through the aspens and cut away pines, looking for the trail Cabe and Cyrus would be taking the horses.

Had no knowledge of this territory, didn't hold no gold or silver in its belly; no trappers, settlers ever ventured into it. It was a kinda lost wilderness fit only for bears, cougars and such. The great forest howled back its defiance, huge trees lashed at each other, their branches flailing out, tearing, cracking, grinding, the great cats, coyotes, wolves, bears, forced their voices up and over to be carried by the wind and lost in the heaving black sky.

The storm gradually rumbled off, coughing and spitting, the sky gave way to dark blue, stars twinkled like they'd had the dust washed off 'em, half a moon slid along, bold and clear. All was deathly quiet up there, leaving us with sound of dripping trees, sucking earth, guzzling the water up like the thousands of thirsty mouths were fighting for it. Dawn showed the torn rain-soaked terrain, its trees near stripped of the new spring glory.

The rising sun's rays steaming the sodden earth causing misty clouds to hover over the carpet of pines, aspens, cedars, oaks, spruce, as we climbed higher, soaking wet, our bellies in need, we rested and munched our meat and bread, got no horse to speak to and Ben couldn't answer, yet his eyes had a kinda grin in 'em and so did mine as we kept moving, our clothes soon drying on account the sun was blasting out its fearsome heat.

Hadn't a notion where we were, which way to go, no Indian trails showed, which told me they didn't reckon the territory offered 'em anything. It was like we were the only coupla living critters 'ereabouts.

For four days we trekked through the forest, sometimes so dense the sun's rays hardly sworded through, the mist still rising from that fierce deluge and we'd soon be out of food.

I gazed over to the distant rims. Nothing showed, not even a finger of smoke curling up into the blue, not a sparkle from a flowing river, just a smooth sea of green, coloured by pines, cedars, oaks, swirling away in the distance. Hope could be right, swallowed up by this savage unrelenting nothingness, a critter could die out 'ere, even his rotting carcass would be a long time whitening in the sun.

For a couple more weeks we watched the days go by, the night sky filled with stars, the moon change its shape, ice cold and indifferent.

The sun burning and blasting its way across the blue, turning the great forest into a waiting fireball, like the slightest movement would trigger it off.

We sure was a sorry sight, ate birds' eggs, Ben snared a jack rabbit when we followed a narrow stream, which we ate raw, making it last 'til it was near maggotty. Got the frighteners when we saw bear sign and heard the great cats, wolves and coyotes howling in the night. Then one morning, coming from thick close low bush, we found ourselves in a dried-out water bed, winding through the green.

It had to lead somewhere, saw horse droppings from wild horses, spied a stallion vanishing into the distant green, got a real good feeling growing in me as our feet rattled through the loose pebbles and shale. A lizard showed itself, which I flattened with a stone. We sat on a baking rock, cut it up and ate it. I'd done such capers before but Ben, his eyes rolled and he gagged on it, but it went down, being only a young'n, sure had the makings of being a man one day living with the right folks.

Hadn't had the notion we were being tailed, but now out in the open could be we'd be seen. Spied a deer, couldn't risk my one bullet on account it would send any curious critters down on us if the shot echoed out all over.

Got mean and ornery, cursed myself for being took by Ringer and Bender, leaving my body so weak, that I'd near ended up with my brains stewing in that Goddamned happy brew, like I was waiting for the Devil to finish me off.

What meat I'd put back on my bones was fast disappearing and my belly began to look like a gaping hole between 'em. Ben too showed his ribs, but he kept right cheerful; maybe he had the Lord in mind like my pard Josh. The river bed tailed off through stunted pines, scrub oak, sparse brush, mesquite, cholla, catclaw and broken rock, massive lumps of it.

Way in the distance against the skyline smoke showed, just a smudge against the blue. My guts gave a tumble, my ears rang. I grabbed Ben and pointed and gave a whoop ... we'd come out of the wilderness, ain't no words for it, just ain't. One bullet and a knife, we'd beat it. Now I was ready for Bender and Ringer, got all the time it takes.

We moved along the burning rocky terrain, the forest becoming a trembling curtain of green behind us sweating under the fearsome heat, bending us over like old men. Heard a distant roar ... wasn't thunder or pounding hooves—it was water.

There was a hurrying in us as we made for it, scrambling over the rocks our parched mouths near stuck together needing to lay our stinking bodies in it, feeling the sound of it beneath our feet. Spied the rim of a gorge, like rows of half-pulled teeth, standing like a barrier, grinning and waiting, pinking in the sun. Had the feeling that watchful eyes were on us as we moved towards it, yet when I looked just the burning emptiness showed.

Lizards, sidewinders and rattlers curled and stretched out, now the early dew and coolness had been taken up.

Our feet echoed between the rocks and outcrops, still had the notion we wasn't the only critters about, a kinda knowing one has when he's been about as long as I have. Saw a bunch of birds wheeling about above the green, then a few more, about half a mile away; saw 'em dip and rise, sure sign they didn't like being disturbed, had a tingling in my body, then we were on the edge. It hung several hundred feet below us, flanked by tumbling broken rock, the water boiled, sending clouds of foam laying over the knife-edged rocks like snow. Its tall sides layered with sparse brush, cactus, stunted pines, swayed in the heat, it smelt like a baking Devil's kitchen.

Eagles and buzzards floated about like brown rags searching for enough air to float up on, screaming and flopping about.

I peered down at the moving water that was like a heaving brown blanket, no doubt fed from the great Colorado River, an awesome sight. I must admit my guts fell low, but I didn't have time to worry about 'em cause Ben grabbed my arm and pointed. Riding out of the glaring heat came Cyrus and Cabe, sitting nice and easy, dangling their long ropes. They reined sharp, their horses stirring up the sand, foam dripping from their mouths; heard their harsh breathing, felt Ben's trembling body. Cabe sniggered, a pleasurable excitement growing in his eyes.

'Seems like you was meant to stay with us, reckon as how you owe us some time to work out on account we gave you three meals a day, ain't that right Cyrus?'

Cyrus nodded. 'Reckon as how young Ben needs a little taming, we folk look after our own, sure do.' Stone-cold, I looked at 'em, their sweaty faces, rotten teeth and dark evil eyes, smelt 'em above my own rancid stink. No doubt figuring on shoving Ben into that shaking cabin and me too, more'n likely, break me in, like one of their wild horses, settle down, like Hope and Abby had so often said. I figured it was time I showed 'em my mean and ornery nature.

My one bullet from that small gun, that had so often nestled between a whore's warm breasts, ploughed through his chest. A crimson froth burst out from a widening hole, his mount reared and bucked, not liking the wet feel of hot blood running down his legs, or the body hanging head downwards over his ass, slowly slipping so the head bashed itself against him.

The terrified animal made off braying into the green. Cabe's eyes turned from me in sheer disbelief. I swung the leather balls just a faint whirr of a bird's wings and they wrapped themselves round his neck. He fell clawing at his throat. I straddled him, tightening the narrow strip even tighter, his eyes popped out of their sockets, his tongue came lapping out, the face turned blue. I grinned at him and waited for his legs to stop kicking and stirring up the dust. I spied his hardware laying a few feet away and was reaching for it when I saw Ben's mouth opening and shutting. Turning, I saw Benjamin and Ebeneza bearing down towards us and a few more from the rear.

Hadn't time to be a kinda hero or wonder if the Devil had given up playing games with me.

'Ben,' I said, 'we're going over the top,' and grabbed his arm. Before he had time to stiffen up at the fearful thought of it I'd flung us over wide. He gave a thin scream, then another as I let go, saw his petrified face, his shoulder length hair swept back, then lost sight of him.

Was aware of the cluttered rock sides slipping by, the brown moving mass below getting wider, the sharp rocks showing wet and glistening; felt the foam on my face as I hit it, falling deeper and deeper, struggling against the heavy swell and suction. Turning and twisting, my head near bursting, I surfaced. Saw his body swirling away, his head bobbing about like a cork.

The deafening roar of it, the mighty force pushing all before it, yet we was still alive, sure was a miracle.

Wasn't no fighting it, just let it take us. Then I was thrust up near him, saw his face change to a kinda grin; we was still together and together we went along. Sometimes on the foaming tips, more often pulled down into its sucking depths dragging at our feet, our bodies rubbing against hidden rocks.

The roar of it, like all the sounds of past yesterdays were being unleashed, as if the evil from that sickening pretty place was following us. I lost sight of him, saw no end, just the moving mass and towering sides as we were swept along.

Then a kinda terror came over me, felt my body losing its fighting strength, my arms and legs getting kinda numb. The water tightened around me, swirling, lifting and I wasn't fighting it, spied him rolling like a log, his mouth opening and shutting. He was shouting, the Goddamn fear of it had unblocked his voice. I shouted back, didn't matter he couldn't hear me. The great roar began to fade, the drag weakened, saw the rocky sides pink and golden in the sun disappear and the great wide open blue sky, holding a blazing red ball, showed itself.

The water ran smoother, still fast, felt a lift, spied him as we were carried on a long tongue, saw him being wrapped round a rock, then half-vanished, felt an almighty crack back of my head, saw the mass of broken rock jutting out like sharp snapping teeth, felt a kinda panic spread through me as I went down, gulping water. Felt the spiteful snarl of 'em like slippery animals with foaming mouths as they threw me from one to another, then an almighty crack back of my head and knew no more.

CHAPTER TWELVE

Wasn't water under my chin, or the sound of it in my ears when I came back into the land of the living, it was mud—thick and warm—my head, shoulders and damn near all my body, lay comfortably in its softness. I looked around, reeds, grasses, coyote willows, silent water and a few yards away, the high blue sky empty of birds and clouds, only that blasting red orb hanging about, scorching everything, drying up the water that had flushed me down 'ere like a floundering fish, leaving me and a few frogs dragging their legs through the mud.

I figured it about midday, then it hit me. *Ben*! I rolled over spitting at the slimy mud, caking my face, no sign of him and my guts sank low.

I got to my legs, sorta soft like I hadn't any bones in 'em, my head kinda dizzy, saw blood oozing over my shirt and fingered that early crack Bender had laid me out with.

Then I spied a shape staggering between the mud and grasses. It was Ben.

We stood staring at each other, then burst out laughing, feeling the mud hardening all over our bodies, like another coat, just our eyes and mouths breaking through ... sure must have been a funny sight.

'We made it Ben, damn right we did,' I said.

He nodded, spitting mud. 'We made it Tobe,' and pointed to his mouth. 'I'm talking Tobe.'

'Yep, you sure are Ben,' I said. 'Been there all the time, just needed a little shove and you sure had it, yep, you sure did.'

We laid in the water and came out near fresh as a coupla spring blossoms, sat on the grass, taking stock as it were, asking ourselves: 'Where was that great roaring river?'

Moved on after a while, spied horse droppings, cart wheels, a few cows munching, patches of ploughed-up land, got a hurrying in us, my legs had bones in 'em, as we came to a homestead.

The heavy timbered house, wide and rambling, stood in a few acres of land backed by willows, cottonwoods, low trees and scrambling hills, streaking away into the distance.

Smoke curled from a chimney, heard a woman's voice humming, the clatter of dishes, the sound of rooting pigs, chickens.

Reckon my head must have bled much 'cause

I didn't see her as she came out just a moving blur, heard her voice saying, 'Well now, bless my soul, well now, you best come right in and sit you down.'

Figured the sides caved in after that 'cause when they slid back again I was laying on a bed.

The room swayed about as I focused my eyes on it. Right pretty it was, curtained windows, coupla pictures on the walls, a few blossoms on the window sill. A small table holding a wash basin and jug, a chair and patchwork rugs on the wooden floor.

I got myself off. My head had stopped bleeding, just a tiny sized lump, which shouted when I touched it.

She came in. 'Well now, it's all right you are, reckon as how you took a nasty crack, had one before by the look of it,' she said.

I nodded. 'Yep ma'am, reckon as how you be right, had a mite of trouble, brought Ben out with me on account he got no ma or pa, ain't no good at reading or writing. Where is this place?'

'Reckon we be about five miles east from where that river thins out,' she said. 'Feeds these 'ere creeks and streams, when it's real high, gets it from that great gorge way out.

'Sometimes this creek holds only about a coupla feet of water then, like now, got more'n it needs. Still, brought you both in and that's somethin' to be thankful for.' She eyed me kinda thoughtful, then shoved my money and

91

notes on the bed. 'Dried 'em out for you,' she added, 'ain't askin' no questions.'

I stared at it, all taken aback. 'I'm right beholden to you ma'am,' I began.

'Reckon as you're goin' to need all the luck there is, got to cursin' a mite you did, that hand ain't for gunnin' yet, you best be right careful, 'cause them critters that did that ain't human, more like rabid dogs.' And she was gone.

There wasn't much of her, small, thin, bunch of grey hair pulled sharp back from a rosy cheeked pointed face, her friendly grey eyes showed her to be a kindly woman. She sure had a lot going for her, heard her feet on the wooden boards, her shrill voice shouting at the dog, snorting pigs and a critter called Jake. I made for the door. Saw my face reflected in the mirror, stubbly black, pale, slit mouthed, ugly, mean, grinned at it, and at Ben standing in the doorway.

'Reckon as how I owe you,' he began, 'ain't never goin' to be able to ...' He stopped.

I grinned. 'Stop your blathering, I figure I done you a right good turn taking you over the top, got your voice back. Ain't that something to tell your grandchildren one day, if ever they believe such a Goddamn yarn, on account we flew down like a couple buzzards? They sure ain't ever going to believe it ... let's go and sample some of that cooking, smells right good, sure does.'

Stayed a coupla weeks with Jake and Sarah Anne, upright, Godfearing folk. Ben seemed to grow tall and muscly almost overnight, talked a lot, to the amusement of Jake and Sarah Anne, but close mouthed about his yesterdays.

They hadn't any young folk of their own and were right glad to have him around. Jake, a well seasoned grizzled critter, had Ben following him about like a dog. Reckon he needed a pa, which he'd never had, someone to look up to, 'cause I'd told him I'd be pushing off soon.

Jake said as how the next town was Longbow, about thirty miles out and Denver about sixty and Boulder County railhead and mining town, with a few fledgling towns in between lay a good eighty miles south-east 'way back behind the hills.

Bought a horse from 'em and, one morning after sun-up, I left.

Felt mighty strange to be on a mount once more. They'd asked me to stay a mite longer and Ben, well, it was real hard, but I had a right satisfied feeling in me; he'd got a chance of amounting to something with these good folks, wasn't a mean thought in their heads. I'd given 'em enough to fix him up with some duds when they next went into town and right funny he looked with Jake's trousers belted up round his waist.

I'd told him to come to Springville in Wyoming one day when he growed up enough, got to be a boy first, then a man, learn to handle a gun and himself, size folks up on account this land was right ornery.

Shan't ever forget him, standing there under the pinking sun, his face crumpling, wet eyed, heard his cracked voice getting stronger all the time. 'Goodbye Tobe. Goodbye Tobe.' He sure had lived a lot in his few years, like me when I'd been a young'n. I turned and waved my hat, felt the horse's hide ripple under my ass, the sun on my back, the nightmare was over.

My mind dead set on getting a pair of .45 Colts, a Winchester and a bowie knife, 'cause I'd got serious business to attend to; heard some geese cackling, sounded like the Devil was laughing with me.

Rode through carpets of sweet smelling sage, sparkling streams, holding large round smooth rocks, like loaves of bread ma used to make. Half-submerged in the water, cottonwoods bunched together like gossiping females, the hot wind whining through their branches.

A few homesteads, peaceful, steers munching away at the tall grasses. Spied chunky humpbacked hills lining along the skyline, ravines, desolate and uninviting, slashed and torn by fierce summer storms and howling blue northerners of freezing rain and snow in winter, now blasted into eerie hazy silence under the unrelenting sun.

Rode out onto a welcoming trail, left by

settlers, overland stage, freighters and such.

Felt a right good feeling reaching all corners as I loped along, my brain racing about like a cornered rat, somewhere out 'ere them bastards were living it up . . . some bastard had his ass on my roan, my friend.

My whole body cringed at the notion of it, felt my bones meet together and the grinding of 'em.

My fingers curled over the palm of my hand, feeling the small hard knot in the middle and not for the first time asked myself if I would ever make it fast enough 'cause I ain't a patient critter, hadn't got time for it, on account the hungry vengeance feeding my body don't breed patience—only a searing hate, like I'd felt when I lost Betsy, watching her die, which is going to take me to the bitter end.

CHAPTER THIRTEEN

The sun was trekking off to the western rims, goldening the distant rolling hills and mountain peaks, giving the tortured land a breathing space, a sorta stretch, on account it had been scorched and cracked since sun-up. Could smell the sear grass, the humid heat laying between the close vegetation, felt it rising up my horse's legs and mine when I rode up a steep grade, sorta getting my bearings. Longbow had to be 'ereabouts and it was. Laying like an old man's greying beard, near flat on the ground in a wide bow-shaped patch of land, flanked by shelves of trees on one side and open going-nowhere land on the other.

A fast-running stream, narrow as a string tie, curved round behind it. Smoke curled up lazily, spreading out, so it appeared larger than it was.

My guts jumped about in my belly and I was for giving my horse a little encouragement when I spied another one, loose tethered under a bunch of cottonwoods, a grey, shaded by patches of black. A hombre had settled himself well down near a dying fire, hat well down over his face, his long limbed buckskin-garbed body, well spread out, his hands no more'n a whisker from his hardware. If he'd heard me he gave no sign, yet I knew he'd known of my coming a long time ago.

I moved carefully through the close brush, loose broken rock and shale, stirring up the dust, which would have brought most critters to life but he hadn't moved.

I dismounted, tethered the horse, wasn't exactly a good beast, after riding a roan, ain't another to measure up to him but I was grateful for what he had to offer until something better turned up; heard the click of metal and saw a .45 pointing to my belly.

'Far enough stranger,' came from under the

hat. The gruff voice and fancy hatband triggered off a memory.

'Why you Goddamn son of a bitch, Thad Oakly—well I'll be doggone!' I spluttered.

He came out from under his hat, right sharp, eyeing me from under bushy eyebrows.

He sure was an odd looking critter, none of him seemed to match, one black eye, one brown, for a start, still had a good crop of brown hair, sprinkled with grey, but right grey bearded and moustached. His long body appeared over-thin, but wasn't, real muscly and hard with it, his weathered seamed face strong jawed and grim mouthed, looked real mean until he laughed; then it oozed plenty of good natured howdys. It was quite revealing.

Used to be quite a man, laying them eager females, had a way with him, sure did, reckon the years must have caught up with him, well turned sixty, leading up to seventy, could be he wasn't up to it, else he wouldn't be lying 'ere with Longbow in near spitting distance. Thadus Oakly, of all critters, 'tis said this 'ere land is full of surprises.

He looked at me, then recalled who I was. 'Tobe, old Tobe, Christ, of all critters, sit you down, you randy old bastard, ain't no Utes out this way. I'll kick the fire into life and make some coffee,' he said, gleefully, eyeing me all the time with them damn odd eyes, his over-long moustache near bouncing up to his

97

thick eyebrows and showing a set of strong even teeth, one any Ute would be feeling mighty proud to have hanging round his greasy neck, which said much on account Thad had been fighting redskins darn near all his life. We sat drinking coffee, he eyeing me out of eyes that should have dimmed years ago, but hadn't, and his body strong boned and well covered held up right well under his fringed buckskin and leather frontier garb. His gunbelt, worn and shiny and a mite thin with wear, held a coupla well-oiled six shooters and no doubt an equally clean rifle deep scabbard over his horse's flanks, 'cause he wasn't a critter who took chances.

Been a frontier scout, Indian scout, rode the great herds to the stockades and railheads in the roaring boom towns and such. Spent time guiding wagon trains of settlers along the great Oregon Trail, safely over the Donna Pass, into the vast untrod territory to begin a new life for themselves and 'ere he was, like an ageing bull not yet ready for putting out to grass. I felt his eyes on my naked body, cause a critter is naked without his hardware and don't reckon on living long without it.

'What's with you then Tobe?' he growled. 'Ain't the same critter I used to know, real hangdog, like you got a wastin' disease. Damn near see your backbone arching up under your jacket, no gun and that poor damn horse, Christ Tobe, had to be somethin' real mean and downright ornery for you to look like this.'

'Yep, real mean,' I gave him and told him all of it.

'Ain't no words Tobe, sure ain't and them ornery bastards roaming all over the territory leavin' their stink to be cleaned up.'

'And you, Thad, what's for you?' I asked.

He lit a smoke, grinning. 'Took a load of settlers along the Oregon, stayed a while, reckon I got itchy feet, more like a ball of tumbleweed, just keep movin',' he laughed, 'had a dozen mail-order brides on one of them wagon trains, ain't never goin' to forget takin' them tight virgins, sure was somethin'.' His shoulders shook at the notion of it. 'Wasn't all virgins time they got there, just a mite loosened up. Right funny it was, had some real good times Tobe, ain't complaining, had more'n my share.'

The fire sparked, we drank coffee and talked of past times when we was young with dreams which most young'ns have, until the fire turned to grey ash and the sun slipping across a sky washed to gold and pale yellow, dipped over the distant western rims.

We rode down the main dirt street of the place, like many more sprouting up in Colorado, on account gold and silver was being scratched and dynamited out by eager-eyed critters who swarmed like locusts across the vast terrain.

99

Some of 'em had dug this stinkhole out and made it look human, holding the usual saloons, whore-houses, eating house, feed and grain, livery stables, blacksmiths, even a row of wooden tubs behind a line of sacking where a critter could lay his sweaty body, lean back, let the water reach up under his armpits and tell himself he was still alive, he'd made it, hadn't been bushwhacked for his horse or duds, 'ere he'd get a belly full of meat, beans, coffee and such, rotgut to wash it down and a woman. Rub shoulders with the thick close bunches of yahooing hombres, stretch hisself a mite after riding hunched up over his horse's head. Yep, made a critter feel right good.

We tethered our mounts outside the Bucking Horse—a rowdy saloon, filled so tight with sweaty hombres, like they all breathed together, holding each other up, 'cause if one was so drunk he hit the floor, most likely he'd never come up again.

We edged through thick smoke and steamy breath, was kinda hard to see the skinny barkeep, looking like a barber's pole on account he wore a rag round his head to stop the sweat from dripping into the rotgut. It was a right pleasing place, no punch-ups, just the idle boastings from 'em, as to how many whores they'd tumbled from one sleazy cat-house to another, sounded like they carried plenty of pollen cause the season had only just got going.

I saw my face in the fly-specked mirror—scarred, straggle bearded, my body sure had shrunk on account my jacket sorta folded loose over it.

We drank slowly, the noise going on all around no more'n a faint whisper for what was beating in my ear drums, Bender and Ringer.

I curled my fingers round the smooth neck of the bottle, my knuckles showing proud under the skin, felt the small fleshy knob in the palm of my hand, cringed a mite, sure I could use a gun faster than most, but being a bounty man, a gunfighter, I'd got to be more'n the best, so other ornery bastards wouldn't be figuring on chancing an early demise, 'cause news moves mighty quick and I'd have 'em sniffing round my ass like dogs, calling me out.

'Reckon I need some hardware Thad,' I said.

He grunted, 'Yeah.' He knew just the place, a gunsmith wedged in between a livery stable and blacksmith. A crafty little runt kept enough in it to fight off a horde of redskins.

Outside the heat and stink wasn't much fresher, just it spread out a mite; in between heaps of garbage, horse droppings, vomit and spittle, drunks lay about between jostling critters elbowing their way along the wooden sidewalks; dogs yelped and lay like curled-up cow pats, a few whores stood around offering their wares, their skirts trailing in the dust. The seething noisy place sure was a most welcome sight. Thad was right, guns that had been hocked by needy critters lay in dusty heaps, rifles, belts, cartridges, knives, the little creep had 'em all. I fingered 'em, smelling the barrels, balancing 'em.

He showed me a gunbelt, holding a coupla .45 Colts and a scabbarded Winchester, smooth, well used. 'Reckon this be what you need,' he advised. 'Belonged to old Jazey Bean, killed enough Indians, bushwhackers and such to fill Boothill on edge of town. Yeah, real fighter was Jazey—dug gold, silver, trapped for pelts in them lonely places, just up and died, all peaceful. I bought his gear and saddle coupla years back, reckon that's all he had to bury himself with, kinda hard ain't it?'

I held the guns, a lump in my throat, could still feel the warmth of those horny hands.

'Reckon I'll feel right proud to have 'em,' I said, 'right proud.' I wound the leather gunbelt round my waist, held the rifle, feeling the worn stock, laying neat and snug and the bowie knife, felt like they'd belonged to me all the time; guess I was meant to have 'em.

We made for an eating house, shoving the thick chunks of meat down our throats like there was no tomorrow.

'Reckon as how you be goin' after 'em,' said Thad.

I nodded. 'I'll find 'em, there's a few more stinkholes like this between 'ere and Denver and always plenty of earholes ready to earn an extra dollar, and my roan will stand out real sharp like a bull without his balls. Won't be easy to sell, a rich man's horse, a one-man horse … won't be hard to sniff 'em out.'

Thad muttered through his whiskers, belching and spitting. 'You just be careful, got to put that lost flesh back on your bones, you just ain't the critter I used to know. Get that hand primed and ready, 'cause you're goin' to need it; reckon I'll ride a while with you.'

I had an urging in me, the next few days, which riled him somewhat, made camp in shady draws splintering the silence with the whine of bullets, spitting and spiteful, tearing at the bark of trees and my cursing and profanity.

'No good Tobe,' he went on, ''til that gun damn near lifts itself out of that holster, you ain't no gunfighter; yeah you can shoot with your left, but this is the one that does the most damage. Them ornery bastards will make buzzard meat out of you, they'll be figuring you ain't got what it takes.'

'Bastard hand, ain't no more doggone use!' I shouted back.

He took hold of it, his thick fingers feeling, probing, grunting and sucking at a wad of baccy.

'Reckon you been mighty lucky your jaws didn't lock together Tobe and this 'ere knob in the middle ain't right, sure ain't.'

103

His wide shoulders hunched over it. I saw the glint of steel, felt a sharp deep dig and before I could buck like a steer with a kicked ass, he turned, a right satisfied look on his face. 'That's it Tobe, never have a gunhand with this in it.'

He held out the black tip of the nail, in between bloody fingers. 'That's what's been gettin' in the way—them doggone muscles been wrapping themselves round it—won't have no more trouble.'

I spread my hand out wide, away from the small bloody hole, the pull was gone. I felt for my gun, resting nice and easy, my fingers closed round the barrel; swivelled it, arced it, wiped the blood from it. A tremendous excitement swept through me. 'Thad, you old son of a bitch,' I got out.

He nodded, enjoying himself nohow. 'Reckon we got work to do,' he growled. He was a right cunning old sod, kept riding me hard, no let up.

For several weeks we rode through harsh baking terrain, no-name trails, where renegades and such slunk like ghosts, mining camps filled with riff-raff, loafers, bums, whisky pedlars, horse dealers and whores.

My body filled my duds, near to straining 'em, my fingers barely left the guns resting in their holsters. I reckoned I could split a leaf in half sideways and grinned at myself in the silent waters, when we made camp. The same ugly mean bearded face stared back, getting more ornery on account I hadn't got a smell of them murdering bastards.

Thad lay back against a rock, hat pulled down, half-dozing, when I spied a rattler only a hair's distance from his neck, tail coming up. Wasn't no time, a bullet tore its head off.

'What the hell Tobe!' he exploded, coming out from under that hat, as the wet bloody head fell onto his neck. 'Christ, that's real good shooting, sure is, the bastard would have done for me.'

I looked at the smoking gun, I'd made it, like he'd said, 'when it damn near comes out on its own'.

The hand and the gun belonged to each other, like it had to the hand which had held it before.

Reckon I'll always have Thad well up in front of my mind; meeting up with old friends is mighty rare in these 'ere parts.

CHAPTER FOURTEEN

It was near one of them half-rooted mining camps, no more'n a few shacks, saloon and such that the Devil showed he still had his eye on me.

Drifting like balls of tumbleweed getting

nowhere, we'd made camp, filled our bellies. It was near dark—no cool air filtered through the trees; could hear 'em cracking, pushing off the baking heat.

Our ears pricked up on hearing the horses' soft blow ... someone was prowling about out in the close green.

We sat quiet, guns ready, on account this 'ere territory swarmed with scavengers, bushwhackers and such.

Thad moved off, quiet as a mountain cat, I edged away from the fire, losing myself in the shadows, heard the roar of a gun, shattering the silence, the shrill whinny of a bolting horse and him booting through the trees.

'Tobe,' he croaked, 'come and see, I done shot a female.'

I saw a huddled body. It had a familiar look about it, my guts sloshed about in my belly as I turned it over.

The leather slouch hat fell off, showing a long narrow face, half-open mouth, broken teeth, the tangled greasy hair tied up in a knot. She moved, her eyes like black stones, sank back in her head, stared at me.

'Abby,' I groaned, 'Abby how come?'

She gave a faint smile, whispered, 'Left 'em after you and Ben went over the top, reckoned you was both dead, followed Ebeneza and Benjamin, killed 'em for what they did to young Ben.' She stirred, moaned and lay back.

106

'I saw you 'way back in one of them minin' camps, couldn't believe it, wanted to see what it's like out 'ere—ain't made for lovin', ain't knowing anythin' about it; had a feeling for you, ain't never had before.

'Reckon I wanted to mean somethin' to somebody, don't rightly know, wanted to have a pretty dress, ribbon in my hair, fancy shoes.

'I been lookin' at them women in the saloons, laughin'—want to be like 'em, I can't ... wouldn't know how.' She stopped, I thought she was gone. She went on, 'Ain't no place for such as me out 'ere, I knows what I look like, just a no-account female.'

I held her close saying, 'Ben is alive and well, living with fine upright God-fearing folk and is talking again.'

She opened her eyes. 'Ain't let the Devil in, Ben's mine, bore him from Old Ezra when I was thirteen years old—misbehaved himself, him in the cabin is Ben's pa, ain't got the Devil in me.' She drew herself up. 'My Ben, my Ben, ain't let the Devil in.' And she was gone.

I laid her back, asking myself how the hell she came to be roaming about, just rags, bone and a hank of hair, yet still in her half-witted brain was a hungry want to be like the rest of folk who peopled this vast untamed land. I reckoned she'd been dodging about like a prairie dog, watching, listening, afraid of it all, yet drawn like a moth to the light; had a notion

107

her short stay hereabouts was the only bit of real life she'd ever had and, like the moth, she'd left it.

We buried her deep at sun up, so no coyotes or wolves would dig her up. Thad got quiet. 'Ain't never shot a woman before, just saw that movin' gun barrel lined up on my belly,' he kept on, like he couldn't shake it off, looking more like Moses than ever. Reckon we both felt it time for us to go our separate ways and at Creaky Joe's stage station we parted, he making for Cheyenne and Laramie before winter set in, leaving with a few brief words.

'I'm an old man, can say old man's things. Go back Tobe, let it go,' and he was gone through the trembling haze, riding tall in the saddle. I missed his great leathery body, deep laugh and the sucking sound of chewed baccy.

Worked my way south past buttes of green, hump-backed hills, plaited and wearing along the distant skylines. Sniffed through more mining camps and cursed at the flaming red ball hanging up in the blue, at its sweltering worst, and at the flies homing-in on my sweaty body, and rode into Rocky Creek, about forty miles from Denver.

A right bustling little place on account a rail spur had lifted it out of the dismals, sported a bank, a coupla places where a critter could bed down without getting his throat cut for a price. A saloon, with a board hanging outside which

108

said 'If yer lost it, don't come back for it' and being as it was punctured with bullet holes, said much for the many irate critters venting their spite on it. I grinned to myself as I loped along the main dirt street, bent on getting a tub of water and a haircut.

The place snored in the lazy heat, like a smoking dying animal, no wind from the mountain tops to take the stink away.

Passing a few drinking dens, a clapboard fronted whorehouse, tethered horses, flicking off bloated flies, clouding up from the dung heaps.

Spied a side street called April, ankle deep in dry rutted mud, a livery stable, sided up between a feed and grain store. Told myself a bank brought many miscreants like bees to a honeypot, had a feeling about the place, which was mighty encouraging. The livery stable was wide, dim and steamy. A dozen near filled stalls lined the sides. A slight sinewy critter showed a flat faced piggy-eyed leathery creep, straw coloured greasy hair straggled out from an equally greasy hat.

He eyed me from snakey hooded eyes. 'You ain't a saddle tramp, snoopin' about where he ain't wanted?' he sneered, from a slit mouth holding half a dozen teeth.

Now if he'd figured I was a passing-through preacher and treated me according I might not have given him my elbow, which jerked him about a foot from the floor, landing him down into a neat pile of horse dung. His face twitched, a rosy glow spread over it and into them snakey eyes.

Loud profanity spilled from his mouth. 'Why you black bearded bastard, I'll...'

'You won't,' I said cynically, 'you just sit quiet while I settle my horse, then I might not rub your Goddamn nose in that heap you're sitting on.'

I threw him a half dollar, settled the beast when I heard a snicker, a whinny, from the end stall.

My guts took a tumble as I went to the end, saw my saddle, my roan.

There he stood, trembling, head down, his flanks showing deep bloodied flyblown welts. His mouth drooled and dripped on account a spade bit, a raised sharp plate, lay across his tongue, a mighty cruel lump of metal to shove into a horse's mouth. I spoke softly to him, eased it from his mouth, washed it out, fed him, squatted in the straw feeling his legs behind my back, heard him gradually quieten, his even breathing.

My whole body cringed at what he'd gone through, a strangled groan welled up out of my guts and the terrible hate and vengeance rushing through my veins shook my bones, damn near heard 'em rattling together. I felt his soft mouth, his breath on my face as I got up,

110

smoothing his hide, fingering the gashes, talking, soothing his shattered nerves.

The stringy creep kept well out of the way as I waited, wet-eyed, and ain't ashamed of it.

The sun had well risen and was riding high when a critter came through the open door, filling out his buckskin duds with a thick beefy body, high leather boots and jingling spurs showed as he made for my horse. Spitting and belching, he reached for the saddle.

'Course he was mighty surprised to see me, on account his pock-marked face turned kinda blue and his eyes, already bulging from their sockets, moved another half an inch. I slapped him hard, heard his neck creak as he jerked back, following it with another uppercut.

'That's my horse you got there and I'm taking him back,' I said, sorta slow like I wasn't in a hurry. Reckon my ugly face and carbon-hard eyes made him more agreeable.

'Paid fifty dollars for him,' he mouthed.

'And that bit and them whippings, they be yours?' I asked.

'So what?' he sneered. 'Goddamn mean beast he is, right ornery, reckon that's why they sold him cheap, the bastard.' He looked at him, adding, 'Reckon I damn near tamed him at that.'

I swung the bit across his jaws, heard 'em crack as he howled and tangled in the straw and waited for him to come up. Strange how the

111

barrel of a gun in a critter's earhole will clear his head, so he thinks kinda straight.

His terrified eyes staring from a red pulpy mass told me he was hearing right, when I asked him who 'they' were and where they'd gone.

Spitting blood and teeth it appeared 'they' had made for Bed Rock a few miles out, another stinkhole along Ceda Creek. I left him fingering his shiny white jawbone and staring at the red stream making crimson patches over his shirt and, telling myself I'd killed men for less, left the place.

Rode my horse loose reined, letting him graze along the streams, talked to him like I used to. I swear that knowing beast grinned back, 'cause he got a gallop going, kicking up his heels like a pesky young'n. Loped through rugged country of stunted pines, close brush, easing off to small meadows, hidden valleys holding wild horses, spied forests of Ceda, spruce like a green curtain through a blistering haze. Followed worn trails and heard the place before I smelt it.

Shaped like a huge shovel it spread itself between high hills, showing gaping holes where critters had burrowed like animals, scratching for the shiny metal. Heard the deafening noise of dynamite throwing giant mounds of earth up like brown clouds in the distance.

Scores of dusty critters moved about in the few streets, holding (thrown up quick!) saloons and such, not a staying place, 'cause when the pickings tailed off it would be left for the whining winds to mourn through its dusty timbers and the grass grow once more covering the brown scab, as if it had never been here at all.

Went into a saloon, ripe smelling and near bursting. Slick cardsharps, snappy and overdressed, flipped the paste boards with their long greedy fingers; even above the noisy clamour it sounded like cracking ankle joints of long horns being prodded up the wooden chutes. The stench from bunches of shifty-eyed critters that found refuge in such places lay thick and heavy. I reckoned there was several thousand dollars' reward hanging over their heads.

A large dirty painting of a near-naked female hung over the bar, dregs of rotgut dripped from it and a few bullet holes let the air in. A sweaty hand pushed a warm beer across the bar, didn't even have a froth on it, but washed the dust down. The barkeep's small button eyes eyed me like he had something right special to say. 'You stayin' long?' he asked. 'Got a few gals upstairs.'

'Nope,' I answered, 'Just passing through.'

He drooped a mite. 'Reckon them cat-houses edge of town, springin' up like fungus, takes all the trade away. Some of 'em females even got tents over by the mines.'

I left him feeling sorry for himself and drifted about the place. Tired-eyed females in their grubby tawdry dresses stood around, sizing up the kinda business riding through the dust and garbage, asking themselves whether it was worth finding enough energy in the fearsome heat to grab what was on offer or wait 'til nightfall.

Found an eating house, a wash house. Feeling sprightly and well-fed began combing the place, having the notion I'd find 'em.

Searching the teeming place, a critter had to have more'n patience and the luck of the Devil.

Spied a crowd of jeering hombres stirring up the dust near a pit of fighting dogs.

Got themselves a reverend, holding forth nohow, hell-bent on saving heathens from the Devil.

A stringy bony critter, wearing dusty black, a stove pipe hat and damn near enough whiskers to deaden his strident mouthpiece.

'You walk in the shadows of evil, there's dead worms in that Devil's brew, it will rot your innards and your souls, cleanse yourselves for the Lord.'

'Reverend!' shouted back a happy drunk. 'You just done me a right good turn on account I suffer from them slippery varmints, reckon I'll have a decent sleep tonight.' That set 'em off yelling and shooting off a few slugs between the skinny black legs of rooting pigs.

114

Was for turning away when I spied Ringer, riding alone.

Felt my sweat turn cold as I followed and watched him go into a whore-house. Wiped the sweat from my hands, as I silently climbed the dim staircase and trod along the landing. Heard muffled guffaws. Bender. I opened the door, smelt his stench, he being a critter who hadn't a liking for a bath or a shave.

His wide back arched as he heaved himself off the bed, matted hair reached up from his belly to his throat, covered his thick muscly arms and thighs, which showed he wasn't an idle boasting critter for all he stank and snorted like a pig. Only thing was when he hotted-up like now he got kinda careless, not hearing the click of my gun—only the stark staring eyes of the woman told him something was amiss. He turned his head, his ugly pock-marked face, fleshy lips, drained near white, as he focused them mean evil eyes onto me.

For a few seconds he tried to pull his brains together, 'cause I must have looked like a dead man risen from the grave.

'It's me Bender,' I said. 'You look real fine, just as you are.' He sagged across the woman, sending a puff of air out of her body; I recalled how he'd always licked his lips over the meaty details, chewing at 'em like a juicy steak.

I put a bullet across his ass, another through his belly, saw his blood flowing over the naked female, who'd got enough wind left in her to let out a scratchy thin scream and grinned to myself as I recalled an old saying, 'keep awake and cautious, you never know the hour or the day when doom will strike'. Old Bender meeting his maker where he always wanted to be ... reckon he was lucky at that.

The shots brought 'em all out from the flea-specked sheets, spied Ringer coming from the dim end, pulling up his pants. 'It's me Ringer!' I shouted. 'Looking up old friends,' giving him time to recognise me.

His snakey eyes widened in utter disbelief and sheer terror, as I sent a coupla slugs through his open mouth, damn near taking half his head off and hightailed it out, leaving screaming whores, booted feet, the smell of cordite and a coupla corpses to clear up.

I rode out fingering the warm guns; old Jazey Bean's hardware had sure measured up right well. I reckon he was hanging around laughing his head off and I was my own man again; ugly, mean and raring to go.

West of the place, steep rockfall reached up into nowhere, pock-marked with holes; to the east shelves of trees formed into thick ridges and a few trails wound like narrow leather strips through the green.

Latching on to one of 'em I made for Denver.

CHAPTER FIFTEEN

It was nearing midday and the blasting orb up high was hellbent on scorching the land to a frizzle and me with it, which set me thinking it was high time I found a shady draw, 'cause my horse was looking more hangdog than me.

'Course, I could have taken one of the trails that had split three ways half a day's ride back and been resting in Hands Cross, a two-bit mining town snuggled between thick browed forestry hills and high mountains, slowly shoving and nudging each other, making fresh thick shoulders, chins and elbows, so a critter had to ask hisself had them new humps been there all the time and why hadn't he noticed 'em before. But I'd taken one of them wide tracks left by freighters, critters on the move and Overland stage.

Sure was busy on account I was always riding in their dust, when out of it I spied a lone rider, trembling under the shimmering heat.

Now ma had been a rare one for words, one of 'em always stands out well in front of my mind. 'Prudent, be prudent' and prudent I was and still am. Closing the distance between us I saw he posed no threat, just a dusty preacher, bent low in the saddle like he was carrying all my sinful ways on his shoulders.

Straggly grey-white hair reached down over his collar. His black coat hung over his stringy body like a limp rag and his thin knobbly knees lifted up his trouser legs, showing ragged socks covering dirty grimy white legs.

'Howdy,' I said. Hangdog he might look. Wasn't dead just damn near baked dry.

'Stranger,' he croaked, 'you be a most welcome sight, to pass the time of day with, yes sirree, a most welcome sight.'

I nodded. 'Well, I reckon we just pull off in that shady draw, 'cause that fireball up there ain't in no hurry to leave yet awhile—ain't doing our mounts any good riding under it.'

His hands tightened the reins. For a stringy critter I allow the large knuckles matched his kneecaps, 'cause they stood up right proud.

We tethered our horses by a silently flowing stream, our fire sent out curling feathers of smoke, birds chirped, bees buzzed and the reverend sat hunched up, hat well down. Reckoned he was near spent and took comfort I could rest easy, wasn't likely I would be getting a knife in my back, him being all-fired on spreading the good gospel words to heathens and lost souls 'ereabouts, reverends being harmless hombres, like jack rabbits and such, don't carry no sting in their tails, just preaching fire and brimstone in two-bit towns, spreading out all over.

'Ain't no settlers or another town for sixty

miles,' I said.

He nodded. 'Rightly so, the Lord's teachings hold a lot of patience, guides us into many strange places and somehow provides, punishing them that mock him.'

'You been travelling far?' I asked, pouring water over my head, enjoying the feel of it spreading into corners of my sweaty body.

'Ah yes, making for Denver,' he said, pushing his hat back, squinting at the sun. Beads of sweat streaked his face, his thick patch of near-white hair stuck flat on his head and ears, showing a right pleasing countenance, rosy cheeked, twinkling blue eyes, a soft smiling mouth holding enough teeth for eating.

The sorta critter a hombre would be right glad to meet up with, on account the territory was thick with renegades, scavengers and such. 'Name's Amos Wick, taking the word of the Lord to all ungodly places, put your faith in the Lord and all is forgiven. Amen,' he said solemnly, then added, 'You making for that heathen place, full of sinful women and devil's brew may the good Lord keep you safe?'

'Yep,' I said, 'then making for Wyoming.' We drank coffee, ate meat and beans. I leaned back and so did my brains, about twenty five years, when I was young and rode with a few critters taking a cow 'ere and there, scraping along.

Digger Bates, the mouthpiece for us all,

Walsh, Boots, Anders, Slim, Stace, me and Knuckles Adams.

Old Knuckles, pulling and cracking 'em like I'm hearing 'em now.

The same smiling face, older, white haired, a right cruel ornery bastard, mouthing the Lord's words like he'd been suckled in 'em. My guts turned over, my hand no more'n a whisker from my gun.

That bastard was up to something, hadn't recognised me on account I'm older, black bearded and mean looking.

Last I'd heard of him, years back, he was working around Corpus Christi, San Antonio and the Mississippi, feeding the brothels with young Mexican gals, snatched from their villages and never seen again. Must be a coupla thousand dollars hanging on his ass for some lucky critter to pick up, but 'ere he was, sitting nice and pretty. Showed he was smart enough not to be worried about a flyspecked 'wanted' notice hanging in some sheriff's dusty office.

'Got a fine horse, stranger,' he said. 'Ain't seen a fine roan for many a year. You been mining?'

'Nope,' I answered, 'sold a bit of land.'

He nodded, his blue eyes sizing me up. Maybe his brain was telling him the horse wasn't his yet, 'cause he settled down, cracking them knuckles and it brought back the time when he'd laughed, telling us how he'd raped and killed a young Indian squaw and kept one of her breasts for a baccy pouch.

Can see the brown shrivelled skin now, as he'd opened it, taking out the baccy, grinning at the thought of it.

I hunched my bones together, all these years and he'd popped up like a gopher out of a hole.

That animal cunning he'd got sure had lasted, else he wouldn't be 'ere now with all his evil ways behind him; wasn't a mark on him, no craggy lines across his face, nothing mean and ornery, as he chuckled and chirped like a bird.

'Sure is good coffee, sure is.' I asked myself where he'd left Amos Wick's corpse ... no doubt eaten by coyotes and buzzards by now. I ain't never been a Lord's man, but don't mean I ain't got a kinda respect for such teachings, for them that gets comfort from them and this murderous hypocrite, filling his evil mouth with sayings from the Gospel book. Just ain't no words for such doings; I knew then I had to kill him. I recalled how he'd always carried a murderous pair of Colts, but 'ere he sat, clean as driven snow, reckoning on his preacher's garb, the Gospel book and his pious mouthings to trap the unwary. The book showed red streaks across the pages, which he quickly closed, eyeing me hard as I reached for a bottle of rotgut.

I saw the avid need for it in his eyes and the quick licking of his fleshy lips. Should I take him now or wait and see what he was up to.

'Prudence' lined up sharp 'cause the situation kinda sorted itself out.

'I feel our paths have crossed before,' he said, reaching over the fire, his hands hovering over a thick flaming bough.

'I shouldn't Knuckles,' I threatened, 'else you're a dead man.'

Kinda stunned, his rosy face drained white, the gentle mouth sagged as he pulled his hand back; his blue eyes turned near pale grey, all of him seemed to change colour and shrink under the dusty black, sweat quickened over his face.

'Who are you?' he stuttered. 'Who are you? You are mistaken, I'm Amos Wick.'

'Amos Wick, my ass!' I exploded. 'You're Knuckles Adams, rode with Digger Bates' gang years ago. I'm Tobe Harris, quite a young'n then; you just cast your brains back.'

He straightened up a mite, figuring he was on safe ground; colour crept back, pinking his face, a sly grin showed.

'That's all right then,' he said, 'seein' as how we got past connections, I'll have a drop of that rotgut and I'm downright sick of this preacher's coat. Goddamn critter wouldn't hand it over peaceable, had to knock him off, figured I'd slide through nice and easy, got a bit of business goin', cut you in.'

I heard the whisky going down his throat kinda slow, wettin' his pink lips and a pink

122

tongue catching the drips, his fingers smoothing up and down the bottle, folding round the bulging sides, a sick kinda look on his face. I figured his thoughts were dead-set on them saloons and whore-houses in Denver.

'What's for Denver?' I asked, full of curiosity.

He sniggered. 'An old pal has settled there, runs about a thousand head of cattle, made a bit of money down the Sierra Madre a few years back. Yeah, we got right mates, with some breakaway Apaches and Yaquis, slipped some gold right under the Governor's nose, on account them generals were wheelin' and dealin' between themselves.

'Maximilian wasn't smart enough to smell the stink risin' about him, heard tell he died without squealin',' he sniggered again, swatting at the buzzing flies. 'Mexico ain't got no Emperor, still it's there, bakin' under the same bleedin' sun, same as us.'

He got more outpourings to get rid of, seems he had to let his tongue wag, that rotgut sure had loosened it. He shrugged. 'It was pretty dicey for a time, things boiled up pretty quick. We split up, never got all I should, 'cause the whole caper turned sorta sour.

'Went roamin', gamblin', whorin', boozin', met up with him in Wichita, sure was a surprise, like meetin' up with you 'ereabouts.' His voice grew cagey, cunning. 'If you was to come in with us, there's good pickings.'

'What sorta pickings?' I asked.

He thought for a minute 'Well my pard's spreadin' out, needs more land, figures on bringin' in another thousand head. Them Goddamn homesteaders won't sell peaceable, hangin' on to them land titles tight as the hair on their heads, sittin' on hundreds of acres of prime land and water. Got to hand it to him, ain't killed any of 'em yet, on account he's made a name for himself, a fine upright critter.'

We both drank, his need for it stronger than mine, making him more eager to let forth his revelations.

'Reckon I might,' I gave him, 'if the pickings are good enough; ain't for killing anyone, ain't so young any more—past forty, don't want no sheriff sitting on my tail.'

'Ain't so,' he snorted, 'I been sniffin' round them homesteaders, got enough loop holes in them land grants and claims to push a steer through, it's all legal trickery. Just means scaring the livin' daylights out of 'em, knock off a few steers, pigs, burn the corn, if that don't give 'em the notion to shake the dust off their feet, well he's all for lettin' it get around, he's bringin' sheep. They'll sell for a few dollars an acre, yep, he's got it all up top sure has.' He belched and choked on spittle and lumps of chewed meat, coming up out of his belly like it had never reached it, laughing and spluttering.

'Yep, they'll be gone before any sheep gets the chance to pull their teeth in that juicy grass, me and you Tobe, just the sorta caper we can handle, ain't that so Tobe? You ain't been featherin' your nest, else you wouldn't be roamin' round these parts, lookin' for the main chance.'

'You sure hit the nail on the head Knuckles, been some time since I had a smell of anything that put an extra dollar in my pocket,' I said.

He sat smiling, rosy as an evening sunset, eyes as blue as the sky and drew out a baccy pouch of wrinkled skin, poking his fingers into it, a lecherous look sweeping across his face. 'Ain't the same one,' he sniggered, 'got this one down in Mexico, had some fine old times down there, Yaqui squaw.' He fingered out another one. 'Apache squaw, right glad I met up with you,' he went on, 'sure am,' adding 'sheriff ain't no help, straight, more's the pity; needs critters like us that don't put a noose round a pard's neck for a few hundred dollars; 'course, a bent sheriff in your pocket, all your troubles be over, killin' him leaves a nasty smell. Yeah, reckon I'm right lucky meetin' up with you.'

I figured he was as drunk as he'd ever been and spat in the fire, sending out grey ash and sparking the wood, keeping my eyes off him, 'cause he wasn't laughing, just digging at my thoughts.

'That's it then,' I gave him. 'I'm in,' near

125

cringing at the sight of him, no more'n the stink of a dead man oozing from him, could smell the sour bitter rancid sweat as he flung the empty bottle, splintering the rockface, scattering blue jays and other chirping birds into a tangled flash of colour up into blue.

I got up. 'Reckon we best be moving,' I said and made for my horse, on account he'd wandered a few yards downstream, a sandy wash slewed off to the right of me. I heard Knuckle's feet in the loose gravel. Like a snake I turned. He stood swaying, smiling, his gun lined up on my belly. 'Don't trust no bastard, Tobe, only myself, you pop up like a ghost from the past and ...' the last words were drowned in a flurry of dust and moving shale, feet first he slid, his gun coming up with a deafening roar, exploding into metal fragments, turning his face into a bloody mangled fleshy ball, screaming in agony he writhed and kicked, then lay silent. The gun had scooped up enough sand in the barrel, splitting it. I reckoned the Lord had evened up for that poor preacher and felt a naked, primitive pleasure running through me, heard the flapping wings of sharp-eyed buzzards hovering above and relished the notion of them curved beaks digging deep into his guts.

Just as well, I told myself, sheriffs ain't partial to bounty hunters riding into town with corpses hanging over a horse's rump, frightens critters away if the place smells too clean, bad for business, makes 'em kinda irritable like they want you, 'be gone, on your way by sun up.'

I got an understanding of them notions and rode off leaving his carcass swelling under the blasting heat, flies already homing-in on such an unexpected feast. I'd let his horse free, after searching his bed roll and saddle bags. Not a sniff who the kingpin was in Denver, just a few hundred dollars. The preacher's dusty black and the bloodstained Gospel book I kept as proof the poor critter was dead.

CHAPTER SIXTEEN

I loped into Denver a coupla days later; it was wide open and booming, trembling under the midday heat.

Been a few years since I'd sniffed round the place, and the great railheads bustling with activity had brought prosperity to it.

There was everything for a critter's needs, from a nail to a pot-bellied stove, calico to fancy ribbons and such, liniments to cure all ails, from the craps to a horse cough. By the look of it a sudden summer flash storm had washed the stink away and seeing the swollen carcasses of dead dogs and chickens shoved under the wooden sidewalks, I figured it would soon be back again. Made for the sheriff's office, strong timbered with a jailhouse clinging to the back of it and another a few yards away.

Spied a schoolhouse in the east corner, sure was an up-and-coming place. I tethered my horse and went into the Sheriff's office.

He sat in a high back wooden chair, a thickset critter with dusty weathered lines across his leathery face, dark brown eyes slitted against the harsh glaring terrain, his hair looked sorta grey on account it was speckled with dust.

The timbered sides were dressed up with plenty of wanted posters holding cunning leering evil faces.

The room heaved in the steamy heat, flies grouped together in the corners, sleeping it off; outside a critter could be swollen up near before he hit the ground if foolish enough to stand around too long.

'You want somethin' stranger?' he growled. I nodded, shoving the note across. He shrugged. 'Another one of 'em—been a long time comin' for it.'

'Yep,' I said, 'had a spot of bother on the way.'

He pushed the dollars over saying, 'Trouble breeds trouble. Still, reckon you can handle it.'

'Knocked off a coupla confederates 'way back,' I said.

He pointed to the sides. 'If they be there you're in luck.'

128

'Ain't there,' I said and shoved the preacher's coat and Gospel book over, adding, 'Knuckles Adams, done killed the poor bastard, you got one for him?'

'Nope,' he said, 'have a swig,' and handed over a welcome bottle of rotgut, his face getting more lines as I told him of Knuckles' outpourings.

'Link Abbot's the only one who's spreading out, putting his fingers in every pie, came 'ere before my time, about ten years back. I got my eye on him, we got a vigilante 'ere and he won't be kickin' anybody's ass. Any land he buys will be at the right market price.' He looked at the preacher's coat. 'Reckon I'll give it and the book a burial, best I can do for him.'

I made for the door. 'Name's Thorne,' he called out, 'Take some of these goddamn wanteds with you when you leave.'

Settled my horse, had a wash, a meal and ambled about getting the feel of the place, heard the distant blast from the thundering belly puffers to the tiny sound of a school bell.

Hadn't set eyes on one this far out and right pleasing it looked.

There was a bit of a ruckus going on between a leathery critter and the schoolmarm. The small crowd faded away as he turned his horse and rode off, a deep scowl across his face.

Wasn't a bad looking hombre, about fifty years old, wore his fringed buckskin and high

129

leather fancy boots like he was used to the better things in life. Suddenly he turned, rode back and sent a coupla shots towards the school house, waited a few seconds, then made off.

She came out, bristling like a polecat, a slight female, about twenty-eight years old, brown hair pulled up into a tight knot, her pursed lips giving her small oval face a right prim look, as did the brown eyes. All of her snapped like a bunch of twigs.

'Well, you seen enough,' she spat and went along a green track to a small house, tethered to the ground by a white fence, a gate and a few steps to the door. I grinned to myself, felt right good, food in my belly, money in my pocket, my horse in good nick, them ornery bastards under the ground, the Devil sure was treating me right after all them backhanders he'd doled out to me.

Had time to think of Jamie, Will and Josh, felt lonely, a need to talk and listen.

The summer had blazed into August and I reckoned to be home before the Fall. Spent a few days idling about, sure needed it, my body lost its tenseness. I no longer felt like a crouching animal, my guts as tight as an iron ball.

Rode out before sun-up one morning. Spied a horse racing along and the flying skirts of a female, then another rider catching up with it. They both reined sharp, she pulled away and galloped off towards town.

Closing in I saw it was the ornery critter who fired them shots wearing the same deep scowl across his face. He eyed me kinda hard, reckoned he'd know me again, 'cause I felt his eyes on me as I loped back.

Passing the schoolhouse I spied her by the open door, shouted a 'Howdy', heard it slam, she sure was a sour gutted female.

Sheriff stood by the open door ready for business. 'You ain't gone yet?' he said. 'This interest you?' and handed me a 'wanted'. A smiling fresh-faced critter stared back, a kinda smug laugh showing the way his mouth crinkled at the edges.

The dusty flyspecked 'wanted' was all of around five years old by the faded wording, 'Buckskin Evans, Knuckles Adams'.

'That's him,' I said. 'Wanted all over the territory, bit of a loner, reward for him being brought in dead or alive around a thousand dollars. How come?'

He shrugged. 'Got me thinkin' when you brought that preacher's coat in, cause a critter wearin' a preacher's jacket knocked off a sheriff in Santos, New Mexico, left a coupla deputies half in their graves, helped himself to abou ten thousand dollars from the bank and vanished a few years back. That's another ornery bastard I can write off the list, only thing is there's always another takin' its place.'

131

I stashed away the money, leaving a live and healthy sheriff sitting in the sun, such critters not given to living long in these 'ere territories.

Later in the day spied the schoolmarm coming along the sidewalk, raised my hat, she stared back.

'Ain't meaning to be disrespectful ma'am,' I said.

She walked on like she was edging away from one of them stinking carcasses under the boards, back straight as a barber's pole, which said more'n if she'd spat out a mouthful of profanity like them frowsy whores, airing themselves in the sun. I grinned, footing it along behind her, she wasn't too skinny, no doubt trim round the legs and ankles, neat waisted, got a bit of shape under that dark grey calico dress, done up high to her chin. Sure wasn't a female hawking her wares about.

Saw her go into her house, raised my hat to the closed door and ambled along to the Broken Spur saloon, filled to bursting, saw the critter who seemed dead set on raising the schoolmarm's hackles. Heard his coarse laughter, was for leaving when he said, 'Won't be long before she comes round to rightful thinkin'; a woman out 'ere alone ain't goin' to make it. Reckon she's mighty lucky I'm offerin' to marry her.'

He drank greedily, his eyes shining bright, quite drunk.

132

Someone shouted, 'Don't you reckon you're in a mighty hurry, Link, on account it's only a few months since you lost your wife?'

He belched, swallowed back whatever had come up, an ugly look spreading over his face.

'Hated me she did,' he muttered, 'then she up and died on me, her starin' eyes carrying that hate to the grave; couldn't bear any young'uns, just never opened their eyes, and she was glad about it. That's all it was, reckon a man wants a woman like he wants his rotgut.'

I went out to breathe fresh air and stop myself from smashing the butt of my gun into his foul mouth. Link Abbot, the ornery critter old Knuckles had reckoned on latching onto for a share of them easy pickings. I figured Sheriff Thorne would see that pot would never come to boil and got real pleasure at the notion of it.

CHAPTER SEVENTEEN

Ambled round a while, then fetched my horse and made for the edge of town.

Kerosene lamps had begun to lighten the shadowy corners and dark wash showed across the paling evening sky, felt a welcome cool breeze singing through the tall grasses as I passed the school house.

Heard voices, hers crisp and cold, his

thickened with rotgut saying 'you shouldn't be ridin' out alone, reckon as how I'll keep you company.'

'When I need it maybe I'll ask for it!' she snapped. There was a flurry of horses' hooves, a whinny, the sound of straining leather.

'Reckon you need it right now, no doggone female's goin' to tell me to shove off,' he snarled.

I heard the sound of a hefty slap. 'You bloody bitch, reckon as how I'll teach you somethin' you ain't had yet,' he laughed drunkenly, adding, 'You playin' a waitin' game, keepin' you awake at nights? Wants to take it while you can, seein' as you ain't been roused yet.'

There was a muffled cry, I rode forward as she broke away, her whip curling across his brutal sneering face.

'Next time you lay your hands on me I'll kill you,' she promised, 'you fouled up piece of human flesh. I'm not like your poor browbeaten wife, screaming and pushing them lifeless babies into the world—get back to the whore-houses where you belong.'

Abbot fingered the rising welt on his face. 'I'll see you run out of town,' he threatened. 'Us townsfolk put up that school house, you can leave it just as quick as you came into it.'

'And I'll do just that,' she shot back at him as he rode off and turned to me, still bristling. 'Well, you another of 'em?' she began.

'No ma'am,' I said. 'Just riding by, figured you might need . . .'

'Don't need anything,' she said. Her hair had fallen over her shoulders like a dark soft shawl, breasts heaved under her dress, her eyes held a sparkle like she wasn't far off crying.

'I'll stay around awhile ma'am, this 'ere town ain't no place for . . .'

'No call for that,' she flung back. 'I can handle it, but I'm thanking you,' and rode off. She sure was a right spunky schoolmarm.

I caught up with him as I rode through the main dirt street, filled with the sound of bustling horsey critters, jingling harness and brawling drunks, the place roared like a well-fed animal. Got a vindictive glare from him, figured he'd know me again and grinned to myself. He sure had got a blistering from that female.

Went to the sheriff's office, collected a few 'wanteds', figuring on picking up a few murdering renegades on the way back, 'cause there was more of 'em about than bristles on a hog's back.

Ain't got no vengeance to hang about for, on account my blood's running clear as fresh spring water through my veins, a racing, a surging, like them birds I see each day, off to distant horizons, over the rims.

Sometimes a critter gets caught in a trap and hurries like hell to get out of it. Been carrying my misery like an extra skin, now I just done shed it, feel light and slicker than a wolf in its spring coat, the past happenings fading away like a night sky.

I rose to a chilly dawn, sure sign of an early Fall and watched the sun rise over the mountain peaks. Being Sunday the town was sleeping off its boisterous goings on, not much movement showed.

Then I saw her, done up in a blue and white check dress with a white ruffle at wrist and neck, a hint of a white lace petticoat peeped out over a slim ankle. Her prim mouth tight-lipped, her brown eyes narrowed, not against the sun, but at him, sitting on his horse.

I heard her shrill voice, carried by a fresh breeze as I loped along.

'You just put your damn ugly tongue back in your mouth where it belongs.' Sure was a mighty funny sight, him all done up in a fancy broadcloth suit, white shirt, knotted string tie and shiny leather boots, like he was off to his wedding, she letting off at him like a spitting cat.

A crooked grin spread over his face. 'You bein' such a smart know-all, with this learning stuff, reckon as how you know too much for a place like this. Got a coupla weeks to get out,' he sneered.

'You finished?' I said.

'Go to hell,' he growled.

136

I shrugged. 'Sure won't get frost bite, I don't like your mouth or the crap that comes out of it—git—on your way.' His face flushed at the sight of my Colt .45 lined up on his belly. He rode off, spitting out a string of oaths and profanity behind him.

She stood quiet, then said, 'You got a name? Mine's Caroline Masters.'

'Tobe Harris,' I said.

'That's it then, seems I'll be getting out, been here six months—could have made a go of it, still, with the likes of him ...' She shrugged.

'I'll walk you back ma'am,' I offered. The sun rose quickly, sending down its fearsome barbs, like red hot needles; shone on her hair, brightening to a rich chestnut.

I reckoned, being Sunday, she'd shed her schoolmarm face, 'cause she smiled, could have been right pretty if she let her hair down and wasn't so Goddamn tight all over.

At her house there was no dallying. She walked up the path, and opened the door, her schoolmarm face back again.

'What's bothering you, ma'am?' I shouted as it closed. 'You shut the door in a critter's face before he knocks on it.'

I roamed about, the town filled up to bursting; ain't slept with a woman since Betsy had died and the sight of them painted whores didn't get my juices rising.

Seemed right and fitting we should meet

again. I'd ridden out cantering through cottonwoods, willows and low shady trees, tethered my horse by a swift flowing stream when she rode up.

Her hair down, divided into a coupla horse's tails, blouse slightly open showed a creamy skin, shiny riding boots pushed out from a buckskin riding skirt, and she wasn't wearing her schoolmarm face. We talked of many things. She'd come from Boston searching for a new life and wasn't finding it.

I let out about losing Betsy and no more. Reckon I looked mean and ornery cause I felt her eyeing me real hard.

Next day I spied her walk past some sniggering whores, back straight, hair up, her dark calico dress dragging in the dust. She stared a mite, made up her mind, and said, 'Cooking a quail later on, if you're passing.'

'Yes ma'am, I'll be thinking on it,' I said.

Sheriff Thorne came riding back with a posse, a string of horses and a coupla shot-up dusty critters. 'Been all of forty miles, nearly into Pike's Peak, getting these bastards,' he shouted, red eyed, sweaty and irritable, as he headed for the jailhouse, hunched over his horse's head, moaning at his lot, sending barbs of profanity in all directions.

I idled the day away, then made for her place. The cooking smells were right pleasing, when I went into the kitchen. The living room wasn't done up fancy, sparse in fact, as if it knew it would soon be empty and it matched her face pursed up tighter than a string bag. She kept her eyes on me as I ate through a mighty satisfying meal, she only pecking at hers.

Then she opened up, saying, 'You carry your bitterness locked up inside, it shows in your sneering mouth, the way you looked at them saloon women and me, like we got nothing to offer—like we're all kinda trash, whore-house leavings. You men never get the notion that we're not exactly taken with you.

'These towns are full to busting with leathery stinking critters with dirty feet and sweaty armpits and nothing to give only a quick tumble under the sheets and not even remembering our faces. Isn't that right?'

She seemed hellbent on bending my ear, as I wiped the plate clean with a lump of soda bread, saying nothing—which got her dander up. Seems she had to let it out 'cause she went on.

'Well I'll tell you something, you don't have to tell yourself I'm a dried-up female with a tight-lipped body to match, waiting for someone to take pity on me, like doing me a favour.'

She walked to the window, her loose-fitting blue homespun dress swirling out behind. 'I'll add to that, I've lain with a man ... been married ... loved ... ah, that surprises you!

'He was a waster, a gambler, a no-good shyster, I see it all around me, but I loved him, with this body, which you no doubt think of no account. I loved him when he got shot up back in Boston, cheating with spare cards up his sleeve.

'This same body ached for the touch of his hands, the feel of his naked body, strong muscly legs against mine. I've got those memories, but I don't let 'em show, I've had the good times, the best, they've gone, not coming back, but I'm not so doggone all fired full of misery that I've written my life off.

'I shall feel like it again and when I do I won't take them yesterdays to bed with me, I'll take the second new experience with both hands, thankful for what life gives.'

My hangdog face, eating blueberry pie, got her more riled.

'Now get out, live with your memories, like wearing a hair shirt, close the door on yourself, mine are like gold dust, never tarnish, or grow old, I need them, so do you.' She stopped. Sure was full of surprises, eager to get her revelations off her back.

I got up, saying, 'I'm thanking you ma'am for the victuals, reckon I'll be off before sun down, no call to shove your grievances onto me.'

We stared at each other, I went out, heard the door shut.

Whatever had been gnawing at her all day, sure had come out.

Did I want another relationship with a woman, on account it had twice ended in tragedy or did I want to drift about bedding whores when the body needed, like she'd said 'not even remembering their faces'?

I was for moving off when the door opened. She came down the path, her hair unwound.

There was a smouldering look in her eyes, her soft lips half-open; had a notion there was a lot of feeling going on in her shapely body. If there was she gave no sign, yet I felt the hunger in her reaching out to me.

'If you come to Springville, Wyoming, ma'am, Caroline,' I stammered. She half-smiled, knowing I wasn't offering anything. 'Maybe I'll come,' she said.

The schoolmarm voice had changed, soft and gentle, it floated on the warm evening breeze, like the smell of her fresh-washed hair and body as she walked towards me.

I nodded, not giving an inch. 'Yep, reckon you'll be right welcome, town's growing all the time.'

'That's settled then,' she said, putting her face back on again.

I felt we were playing a silent battle, a warm excitement spread through me. I rode off, saying nothing, felt her eyes on my back, still feel 'em as I make for home and Jamie.

It was at Snake Head Pass I knew I had company.

Was for crossing a stream when I saw Link, standing on a spit of land in the middle of it, a wolfish grin splitting his face, his gun lining up on my belly.

'Course he shouldn't have been foolish and foolhardy like wanting me to know I was for buzzard meat.

I put a coupla shots through his kneecaps. 'Ain't for killing you,' I snarled, 'just that you're going to walk mighty crooked from now on.'

He fell back with a terrible scream as I rode off, leaving him threshing about in the reddening water.

He sure was a lucky critter, me being in a pleasant frame of mind, which I ain't very often. Could have killed him, he sure was lucky.

The shots hadn't disturbed the quietness, no birds tangled up in the paling sky. Reckon my roan has the same hurrying in him as we move through the green ... figure he knows we're heading home.

Photoset, printed and bound in Great Britain by REDWOOD PRESS LIMITED, Melksham, Wiltshire